O, My Word

O, My Word

Ina Hughs

Faraway Publishing
Black Mountain, N.C.

When I use a word," Humpty Dumpty told us in rather a scornful tone, "it means just what I choose it to mean—neither more nor less."

Table of Contents

Foreword

When my children were in elementary school, their vocabulary textbook was called "Wordly Wise," and each Friday they were tested on the dozen or so new words for that week. They had to spell it, give its definition, and use it in a sentence. Something like that happened to me after learning from a friend taking art classes about a practice assignment they were given—a list of random words. They were to do a simple sketch off each one of those words. So I started collecting words. Friends, family, my book club, my discussion group, I asked to choose a random word, and I would write based on that word. The word became the title of the piece. Mostly stories, mostly fiction, mostly short.

Radiant

It was late Saturday afternoon. The sun was chased down by gray clouds, and I heard thunder roll over the mountain as if to warn me. We were in the living room, me listening to the Yankees and Los Angeles Dodgers battle it out, and my wife Jan, stretched out on the sofa, reading a *Country Living Catalog*, and saying something about a cute little red polka-dotted mushroom spoon holder with matching salt and pepper shakers she might order. "Mm hum," I mumbled, half-hearing, not even trying to imagine a mushroom salt shaker or to admit to my wife I had no idea why a spoon would have to rest.

It was the bottom of the 6th, score tied. The crowd was wild, but during a commercial I noticed the room was quiet as a church. I looked over at Betty. Her arm had slid off the sofa. The catalog was on the floor. Her head was down on her shoulder. She wasn't snoring.

Grief is like the wind. It can blow you away. It can rush through well-meaning words, snuff them out. Grief can drive you crazy, as the wind did pioneer settlers out on the Kansas plains trying to maintain sanity. Like a storm pounding outside the window, grief can bang against you like a devil spirit.

We did all the right things. Church funeral with a sign-in guest book; everybody got a handwritten thank-you from me or our daughter Elizabeth. Neighbors brought fried chicken and potato salads. We ordered the headstone. Betty and I both had wills and all that business, but she did not want to be cremated, and I do not want to lie in a box for all eternity. That was the only important thing we ever disagreed on. Betty's sister and brother-in-law invited me a least once a week to come stay a while with them, but I knew I wasn't good company.

That was 25 years ago. I'd never lived alone before, but I managed, even the grocery shopping. I saved coupons, looked for bargains, stuck to generic brands, except for ice cream and organic eggs. I had my golf game every week with church buddies and took on being program chair for Kiwanis. Elizabeth and Charlie eventually had two children. They call me Grandpoppins.

Now old age shows up like an uninvited guest who complains all the time. It constantly barges into conversations, cramps my style. Bones creak. Feet swell. I buy a recliner, wear orthopedic shoes with elastic strings, and sometimes forget to bathe. All music on the car radio gives me a headache. I sleep in socks.

And recently I've been seeing Betty. Really seeing her: in the backseat of the car, standing outside in the rain, waiting in the pharmacy line, and last Sunday when I stood for the *Gloria Patri* at church, I saw the back of her head two rows in front.

I haven't mentioned to Elizabeth that her mother is stalking me, nor have I consulted a doctor of psychiatry. I am positively sure of two things. I am not crazy, and it is Betty.

So next time I see her off in the distance, I will go to her, hoping she opens her arms. And that's what happens, of all places, in Anderson's Service Department, while my Rav 4 was getting its 90,000 mile checkup. There she is. My Betty, sitting by the free coffee table. Just as I stand up, I lose my balance as a monster fist digs into my left shoulder, leaving me slumped sideways back in the chair. I hear the ambulance and see the EMTs rush in with their hand pumps and stethoscopes.

Then I see Betty coming towards me. She calls me by name, she takes my hand, and in an angel's breath, we both rise up above the chaos in the room: a newly radiant couple holding hands and heading Home.

Crush

When my daughter Amy came home from her play date with Sarah Hunter, she announced at supper that night she'd decided what she wanted to be when she grows up. Her dad and I never asked that question before, but we knew it was a staple of childhood, right along there with "What are you going to be on Halloween?" Amy was in second grade now, so I guess time had come to start thinking about such things.

"What? Are you going to be?" we asked.

"A gladiator."

"A WHAT? " we both spat out at the same time.

"A GLA-DEE-A-A-TUR. You know" . . . and with that she stuck out her chest, picked up an imaginary sword, and thrust it with a growl, almost knocking over a glass of water.

We were speechless.

"I'm going to defend myself from lions they let out in front of the crowd in a stage-like arena with fallen-down stone walls all around, and people called Imprers and Romints shout and cheer from their seats," she went on, while we stopped eating so as to not miss a word.

"The lions will all be killed when they fight me, but if I was fighting criminals—a lot of criminals ended up being made to be a gladiator, and when all the lions were dead, they had to fight each other. I wasn't ever a criminal, don't worry. I am a nice person who just volunteered, so when I have to fight real people instead of the lions, I'll just stab them gently somewhere safe, like the ankle or elbow, and tell them to play dead or else . . . . ."

Who was this child?

She went on to explain that blood and guts might make her throw up at first, but she'd get used to it! Doctors and soldiers have to.

Oh my Lord, I almost said out loud. Does Amy need therapy? Do I need to take it to our pediatrician? How can I be supportive? There aren't any gladiators for hire in 21st Century USA, and where did this fascination with violence come from? Are we going to be one of those parents whose child never leaves home and must be supported on retirement savings? Where did we go wrong, and what would a child psychologist say if his sweet little 8-year-old had her heart set on being a gladiator?

I remember having a crush on Hopalong Cassidy when I was about Amy's age. I dressed like him, tried to walk like him, bought his comic books. But I never wanted to be him. Besides I have always been terrified of horses . . . the way they go up on their hind legs.

Amy was now looking expectantly at us: first her dad, then at me.

"Amy, sweetheart," her dad said, "people aren't gladiators anymore. Where did you get this idea? Even thousands of years ago when there were such things, I never heard of any female in the Roman Empire."

That actually wasn't true. I Googled gladiators after supper. There were gladiatrices, as they were called, and I won't describe my nightmares after seeing the creepy gladiatrix paintings on Wikipedia: my sweet baby darling in a canvas loincloth and a peacock feather helmet. Size 7.

Well. That was that. Now, a year later, she no longer sees herself in the Roman Coliseum. Now in third grade, she's trying to decide between a Dallas Cowboy cheerleader and a Baptist missionary.

Toad

Whoever in fairyland dreamed up the idea a toad would turn into a handsome prince, if you kissed it, was not the brightest crayon in the box. In the first place any girl who would kiss a frog had to be really hard up. Think about it. The monster-long tongue with leftover fly parts stuck to it. And why would any decent prince be living inside a frog? Or a toad. How'd he get in there? When something comes out of something else, the two something's share family resemblances. A prince of that nature could've, and by the laws of physics and all other "ysics," would've had features akin to its deliverer. Can't you see it now. A homely, disturbed maiden picks up a toad and decides to give it a smooch. Out jumps a man-frog, with dry leathery skin and large bumps; huge, glassy eyes that don't blink but once every half hour, that speaks in burps. That girl, no matter how horny, would run like hell.

Friend

Gerald Huntington is an ordinary man, sensible, frugal. Not somebody to notice: mostly bald, face pock-marked but fastidiously shaven, medium height, medium weight, medium looking. Gerald Huntington is medium.

Retired from an accounting firm, widowed ten years, he lives in a frame house with a backyard that blooms year-round in perennials of the season: weedless beds behind meticulously placed bricks, same color and size. An old, off-balanced swing haunts the far corner of the yard, since the children grew up.

Every morning at 8:00 Mr. Huntington drives to the McDonalds on Crescent Avenue for a medium coffee, black, one sugar. Mrs. Huntington prefers tea and thinks it silly to perk a single serving in their 12-up Mr. Coffee, so this was his schedule every morning for over half a century, and he is a man of unbroken habits. One day he notices a man slumped in a folding chair in the median at the crossing light where Wagon Trail meets Crescent. Has that man always been there?

Two weeks later, he's still there. Same time. Same man. Same spot. Just sitting. Not begging. Never jumping up to wash windshields for a handout when traffic stops. He has a thermos, sweater on, sometimes off, depending on the weather. And always, always an earnest look on his face.

Mr. Huntington is not a spur-of-the-moment person, but one day he pulls to the side of the road and gets out. Why not? What else has he got to do? The hedge is clipped, bird feeders full, and going to the grocery store would be just an excuse not to head for his La-Z-Boy and watch TV commentators stomp and shout all the ways America is falling apart.

"Hello there," Mr. Huntington says, trying not to look foolish.

For what seemed like hours, they chat about the weather, the traffic, the makes and ages of cars stopped at the light. Finally Mr. Huntington asks, "You from around here?"

"I live about half a block off Glenwood. You?" the man answers.

"We've been in this neighborhood over half a century," Mr. Huntington explains. "My wife died a while back, but I stayed right here where we raised two girls and a menagerie of cats that didn't have sense enough to stay out of trouble . . . or the street." Mr. Huntington surprises himself at how easily he slips into small talk. He isn't a chit-chatterer.

That's how it started. Morning after morning Mr. Huntington drops by on his way home, and they talk about the rising cost of plain, everyday white bread; about different places they'd lived; about gardens and grandchildren; the Braves and the Cubs; about how boring Sunday afternoon golf is. Almost a full week goes by before they mention names.

Gerald Huntington. Bruce Statelier. Next day Mr. Huntington brings his old fold-up camping chair.

Mr. Statlier had been a school principal out west and worked as a Habitat volunteer until his knee went out. His son served in the military, but he never mentions much else about his family. Mr. Huntington tells story after story about being on the City Council years back, how naive most people are about money and budgets and owning credit cards. It never occurs to either to ask personal questions—two old men sitting in plastic chairs at a busy intersection, watching traffic.

One day in the middle of a conversation about the woman who went over Niagara Falls in a barrel—crazy thing—a policeman pulls over, gets out, and heads their way.

"How you doing these days, Mr. Statlier? Haven't seen you in a while." The policeman drops to his knees on the grass and waits for an answer.

"Doing better, sir, and I want you to meet my friend Mr. Gerry Huntington here." It's obvious the two of them know each other, but neither brings up when or how. Instead, Mr. Statlier asks the patrolman did he ever hear about a woman who supposedly went over Niagara Falls in a wooden barrel.

"Oh sure," says the policeman. "Famous story."

For ten minutes they hear in detail about how she was 63 years old, ended up with only a nothing-scratch on her forehead, and told the newspaper reporters afterwards she'd go stand in front of a fast-moving train before doing such a fool thing again.

The policeman looks at his watch: "Hey! I gotta get back to work," and off he went.

Neither man says anything until Mr. Statlier turns to Mr. Huntington: "I want to know why you come here every morning?"

Gerry Huntington himself wonders why he pulled over so many weeks ago and started up a conversation with this stranger: 'It just felt like something I needed to do. An unfamiliar impulse I guess you could say.' He admits he'd driven by a dozen times before he stopped, looking for hints as to what the man was waiting for. Was he homeless or injured? The mystery was in the look on his face. It never changed. Why such a serious expression?

Traffic comes to a standstill. Mr. Huntington wants to avoid more questions, go back to regular-type conversation, like why some people blow their horn when there are 20 cars in line at a red light. Or why women drivers lean forward and men sit straight as sticks. What makes a person put bumper stickers all over the back of the car?

Bruce Statlier turns his chair to face Mr. Huntington and tells his story. "I had a son in the Marines who was killed some years ago in the desert. His name was Andrew, but it got shortened when his baby sister couldn't say "Andrew." Yes, Drew had a younger sister. Her name was Julia. When Drew was in ninth grade, he got mixed up with a rough crowd. His junior year, Drew dropped out and did nothing but drink and drive fast cars. How did he support himself? Shoplifting. Running drugs. Housebreaking. Fake credit cards. Calling old people, pretending to be from Social Security. At nineteen, he was arrested and spent nearly a week in jail. A sympathetic judge gave Drew his last chance to clean up and stay out of trouble. So he joined the Army. Two nights before leaving for basic training, he and Julia were driving home from a farewell party for her brother when their car was T-boned by a moving van that hadn't slowed down at an intersection. Julia died instantly. Drew was unscathed."

After a long silence he continues. "When Mildred and I arrived at the accident, I lit into Drew like a raging bull. I knew for certain he'd been drinking." Here Mr. Statlier stopped, then, almost in a whisper: "I lost my temper and said awful things, the kind of things you try to take back but hang in the air between you forever. That policeman you met today finally calmed me down. Drew left that night and said he was never coming home. When he didn't write or call or come home on leave, his mother blamed me and things went south in our marriage."

He looked back over his shoulder: "This is where it happened. I lost all of my family right over there. This intersection where we sit. Julia was killed on the spot; and Drew, I think, by choice not long after. Mildred never recovered from the stroke she had that same year. I take the blame for the anger and grief she stuffed inside."

He stood to finish his story: "A day later, two Marines in full dress stood in our doorway, telling us Drew had volunteered to sneak up to the bunker where enemy fire was coming from. He didn't make it. He stepped on a mine. Mildred and I—the four of us—stood in awkward silence. 'You and your wife, sir, should be extraordinarily proud of your son. He is a hero.' They gave a sharp, slow salute and then were gone. My wife put her face inches from mine and with a force so strong that spittle came out of her mouth she yells, 'I blame you for this' . . . . Drew did come home then in a flag covered casket, buried next to his sister . . . and not long after, his mother."

Gerry Huntington and Bruce Statlier continue to meet every morning in their two chairs until road construction drives them into McDonald's. One day years later Mr. Statlier stops showing up. They'd never exchanged addresses or phone numbers. Mr. Huntington waits for weeks before he decides to believe his old friend is reunited with his family, happily making up for past mistakes, for lost and stolen time.

Ice Cream

Bethany Neilson goes to bed every night with Bobby Flay. Well, not *with* him, but lights off, she watches his show on her iPad she has propped on a pillow by her head. "Beat Bobby Flay" is a Food Channel competition that comes on MAX, and there's something about pan frying, sautéing, boiling, cutting, mixing, and plating that numbs her mind. It's like a lullaby. You could say Bobby Flay is her Sandman.

It's odd she's so taken with a food show because Bethany never cooked. She wouldn't know a crouton from a hockey puck. Her mom fixed their meals. In college she ate in the cafeteria, and now her apartment kitchen is where she keeps her two black labs and their food dishes, water bowls, and dog beds, so until she started dating Jake, she ate frozen dinners from Kroger. Jake, as it turned out, is the executive chef in a snazzy high-end restaurant with a French name she can never pronounce right: Tutuaylachey or something like that.

Then Jake asked if he could move in. Her secret was out. He had always brought over leftover stuff from the Tutulacey-whatever, but who wants to eat cold anchovy tartlets at 6 am? She didn't even know how to make coffee. Jake had a nerve-out that she used K-cups.

All this is to say, Bethny went to Barnes & Noble to buy a *Joy of Cooking*. She hoped the "joy of" would come later, but at least now she had some recipes. The new Mr. Coffee came with pictures on how to use it, and the internet clued her in with measurements and water levels. Next? How hard can it be to boil an egg and spread butter on a bagel? There was always cereal. Open box. Pour milk. Piece of cake. She had breakfast covered.

Other meals, not so much. She asked Jake his favorite sandwich and didn't hear one recognizable word, like jelly or head lettuce, in any of his choices. His very favorite, he explained (and I quote) " . . . gilded in 24-carat-gold French pullman bread made with Dom Perignon Champagne, covered in grass-fed white truffle butter and filled with slices of Caciocavallo Podolico cheese." Bethany's first thought was, "How does one feed grass to a truffle."

The *Joy of* Cooking suggested a good meatloaf is hard to mess up, and with mashed potatoes, all you need is a potato and hand mixer. So that is what she'd fix for their first meal, but it turned out, even with the book right in front of her, it got depressing. What is *al dente*? What do teeth have to do with potatoes? Bethany had no idea ground beef could get so complicated. She was getting TMI from details of selecting the right cut. Reading aloud here: "The meat industry includes the slaughtering of animals. The process generally includes stunning, bleeding, eviscerating, and skinning." She thought she was going to upchuck. "Carcasses are then inspected," it went on to say, "and graded according to government-set standards of quality."

Wasn't "best by" just a suggestion. What if your meat was bought on sale the day after the label date (that's why it was one sale) and your dinner party was on the day after that? Would your lips swell and your bowels explode? She wished Jake was a vegetarian. Maybe they'd have a hearty salad and nice bread instead of meat and potatoes. She began another shopping list, but then the doorbell rang. It was Jake, and he brought some *Coq au Vin* for a late supper. She was scared to ask what it was. It sounded suspicious.

After Jake left, she was too tired to think about the grocery list, so she and Bobby Flay went to bed. Before she fell asleep, Bethany was thinking why not just play a segment of his show in slow motion (stop & play) and mimic exactly what he did. Or maybe, she could run in a good seafood restaurant and buy their special and side already prepared. For dessert, she'd go with Häagen-Dazs Swiss Almond Chocolate. Beats well-fed truffles every time!

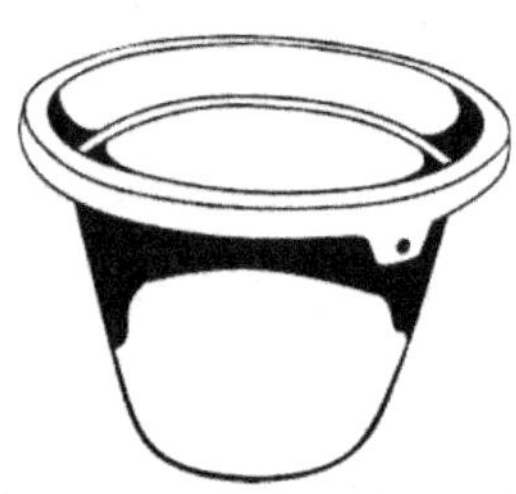

Mind Games

Pam woke up before her dream ended. With half-closed eyes, she looks around her room: the bookcase with her *Hitchhikers Guide to the Galaxy* series, the crocheted blanket her grandmother made, the yapping of their neighbors' annoying mud-colored Rottweiler. But the dream stays inside her head, and she shuts her eyes. She doesn't want to come out of it.

Tomorrow she is leaving for a month at sleep-away camp. She's never been away from home. Nobody has ever asked her to a sleepover. Her grandmother lives in the same town. On a church camping trip with middle-schoolers she came down with a bad stomach ache, and her mom came and got her. She spends most weekends babysitting her two-year-old brother.

In the dream, she is at summer camp on the top of the bunk bed she shares with her new best friend, Cheeto. The girl's real name was Cheryl, but Cheryl is quick to earn the nickname because she can eat a whole large-size bag of Cheetos in one rest period. Everybody has funny nicknames at camp. Worm (as in book). Giggles (obvious). Zac-Econ (a mad crush on Zac Efron). Honey bee (what her dad called her when they said goodbye that first day). Blondie (she had the jet-blackish hair anybody'd ever seen). Pam loves her nighttime dreams about what life is going to be like at Camp Green Cove. Her nickname is Poppsie because she is so popular. Everybody likes her. Everybody wants to be on her team, to sit with her at lunch, to play Slap Jack or Gin with her on rainy days.

Home is so different. She has no school friends. She was a nerd from the very first.

Clumsy. Too fat. Wrong clothes. And when she is upset or anxious—who wouldn't be in her shoes?—she can't think of anything clever or remotely interesting to say. And bullies zoom right in on those kinds of silent, head-hung losers.

Maybe Green Cove will be different.

Footsteps

Have you ever found yourself in an empty parking garage late at night. Your car the only one. Overhead lights flicker a few times, then go out. Not far behind you, the elevator door opens. You hear footsteps. Closer. Closer. Then the inhuman snarl, the heavy breath of something at your neck. Time stops. You try to scream. A hideous claw-like hand grabs your shoulder, another reaches for your waist. A dry tongue slides down your cheek, under your jaw. Then something of a hiss before this creature, this beast, this monster pulls you down to your knees, and in the sucking darkness your whole life passes before your eyes. Have you ever? Did you ever? Me neither.

Pine Cone

It was on a Sunday night at church camp that Mary Dalton realized she might be an infidel. At vespers that night the visiting missionary said not believing in God was the worst in the world, the only sin that God couldn't forgive. After that everyone sang "Just as I Am," and Mary snuck out, walked to the edge of the lake, and sat on the porch of the canoe shed to think.

The missionary said a born-again believer, the only kind that gets to heaven, had to take the Bible as exactly true. Mary was pretty OK with most of the New Testament, though she had to suspect there was something fishy in the feeding of the 5,000, but she knew people tended to exaggerate retelling exciting stories, especially ones that involve numbers. She and Buddy once had a contest to see who could put the most Double Mint gum in their mouth at one time, and he won. When he'd brag about it to his friends, he swore it was over four packs. Mary knew for a fact it was only two and a half. She was there.

The Old Testament scared her as a child, and even though she was fifteen now, it scared her still. Tonight she realized those prophets and disciples who wrote the Bible would put her on the infidel list. So would tonight's missionary. It seemed to her that God had a split personality. There was the one that put Moses in the bulrushes and saved him from a horrible fate, the same one who compared Himself to a shepherd, the one who let David beat up Goliath.

How could that be the same God who drowned all the people and animals except those in the ark. And what about Job? Over years of Sunday school Mary heard the Bible stories; then there was vacation Bible School. Mary remembers the summer they built a big cardboard boat, and everybody made clay figures of their favorite animal twosomes and walked them into the ark. What about the rest of the animals? And people outside the Noah family? They drowned, too. Never heard of again. And there was the Jonah coloring book that had page after page of his being swallowed, him inside the whale, and of the miraculous spit up that landed Jonah on the sandy shore. Dicky Maddox asked why crazy things like that never happened anymore. She wondered, too.

Mary decided to think about something else, but her mind was busy trying to sort her feelings. Did she really believe in all the Bible. Was God really real? Mary decided to settle it once and for all. God, if you are really real, just this once please prove it. Maybe she should say it out loud. "God if you are really real, make that pine cone over there turn over. The one just there off the porch. That pine cone. Turn it over."

After Taps that night she felt something inside her was missing. She had waited for almost an hour, but the pine cone didn't move. Not once. Not even a tiny bit. Maybe it moved in the middle of the night, and she wasn't there to see it. Does that count? Mary finally fell asleep, but not before deciding to give God one more chance. Yes, that was it. Patience is a virtue. She'll keep looking for signs. Which she did for the rest of her life.

Quirks

Charlie came into the world hating water. He screamed bloody murder when his mama gave him his first little sponge bath in the litter-box sized plastic tub from a baby shower. But Charlie turned blue with rage, so mom gave up and rubbed him all over with antibacterial hand wipes while she sang about the Little Pufferbillies down at the station.

Charlie was an easy baby, but he simply wouldn't tolerate baths. This went on for 3 years. At 4 years, she tried putting her feet in the water, hanging her legs over the tub; maybe that would help, but he got so terrified he scratched and fought until mom herself panicked and Dad came running to the rescue. When Charlie turned 5 they bought an outdoor baby pool and tried playing splashing games to get him to join in. He didn't.

Now Charlie was 6. Too old for such nonsense. They talked to the pediatrician about Charlie's paranoia. And the doc said it was a little unusual, but just take it slowly, maybe throw in some toys, make a game of it. They agreed. Charlie would get over this problem eventually. Although she was philosophically opposed to bribing kids with toys, she researched Google to learn what toys were psychologically best for bath-time and also kind to the environment.

She gingerly put Charlie in the tub that had yet to be filled with water. Then set the faucet on the lowest drip, drip mode and put the stopper in. So far so good. When the water formed the tiniest puddle around Charlie, she handed him the iconic bath toy, which, according to Wikipedia crossed all ethnic and cultural bases as the best bath toy. A rubber duck. She had been warned against the popular yellow duck because kids didn't particularly respond to yellow. It was too subconsciously linked in their developing minds to aggressive house cats, lightening, and summer squash. Green was the most non-threatening childhood toy-color according to pediatric research at Harvard's School of color psychosis in pigment transference in early children. Yet, Charlie didn't hold the green duck long enough to discern its color or have any transference. He just threw it across the bathroom and tried to climb his way up the side of the tub, falling face down in the slippery porcelain.

It was a trying week. Every night she set him in the tub with half an inch of slow-drip and tried a different toy: a pink squeaky pig; a tiny rubber gecko creature the color of flesh; a plastic boy-child that looked like Charlie himself, and finally a purple circus mouse dressed up in pearls and lace. All ended up on the floor of the bathroom with Charlie in a scrambling-out rage. So much for the toys. Next Mother tried bubble bath, but that was worse because Charlie hyperventilated in such a panic Mother was afraid he'd ingest so many soap bubbles his lungs would burst. "I GIVE UP!" she said, leaving the bathroom, carrying a sobbing, slippery-wet Charlie.

Father heard the ruckus and came to the rescue. He slapped her on the back in his buck-up, get-a-grip, put-on-your-big-girl-pants way of empathizing: "Let me handle this. You stay out."

And she did, but she simply could not tolerate the noises coming from the bathroom. Screams. Shouts. Splashing. A deep adult-male gurgle. And cursing. And all the while she heard Charlie move from whimpers to bawling, then nothing but pitiful hiccups.

Father came out of the bathroom looking like he'd been the loser of a two-hour underwater special on Wrestle Mania.

Charlie never had another tub bath, stall shower, hosing down again in his entire life. Even as a grown man he only used a wet wash cloth to clean up, and somehow he managed never to look shabby, never had body odor, and, you might find it hard to believe, but Charlie was fussy about his hair, and who would ever believe a normal looking human being can always look immaculate when he bathed with Wet Wipes and washed hair with dry shampoo and a hand towel.

Coincidence

Competitive sports are not all trophies and cheers. Playing can be deadly. But Sue Lynn McNally is the only person in all of history who was killed playing dodgeball. Football players get cleated and knocked senseless. Basketball players split kneecaps or crack skulls. Tennis and golf sound tame enough, but what if a ball going 120 mph slams into your temple? Dodgeball at recess, isn't that 100% pure safety? Skinny 5th and 6th grade kids can't throw a big soccer ball that hard, and besides, everybody sees it coming so they . . . well, they dodge. Only Sue Lyn didn't. It somehow got tangled in her legs, she fell backwards and ruptured her spleen. Randy Clemons who had thrown the deadly ball yelled, "Gotcha, Lue Synn NcMally. You are O-U-T."

Sue Lynn didn't move, eyes open all glassy-like. Was she faking? She wasn't. The next scene plays like a high-speed movie: the stretcher sliding into the back of an ambulance; red droplets in the grass where she'd landed; our parents called in sing-song beeps on the policeman's radio phone. Twenty-three years later, by some crazy demented coincidence, that same Randy Clemons turns out to be the phys-ed teacher at my daughter's middle school in Potsdam, N.Y. Randy has her playing Roller Bat. Red Rover. Capture the Flag. Annie Over. Kick the Can. Red Light, Green Light. Tug of War. Sling the Statue. But no Dodgeball.

Pizza

The college counselor at my high school is a dork. Hunched over her desk, she nods at everything I say, and if I don't say anything, she just hunches. It is ridiculous. College Counseling is required every winter quarter for all 11th grade Students Who Show Promise. She didn't ask if I even wanted to go to college. She assumed. Truth is, my father would have a cow if I opted out of college. I'm an only child. He has big plans for his son. I was thinking maybe UGA (go Dawgs) might work, but it isn't in the batch of brochures Madam Hunch picks out after consulting my teachers. "How about Princeton?" she mumbles. "Or maybe Yale." Too far from home. "M.I.T.?" Too expensive. "Morehouse?" Yeah, Miz Hunch-Mumble, like I am going to an all-men's school. Not a chance, sweetheart. I didn't actually say that out loud. So, we sit there. In silence.

By now I too am hunching. I could tell the ball was in my corner, so I ask what did she think about Shanghai Jiao Tonga University. At that, she un-hunched. "Say what?" I tell her it has a great Biomimicry department.

Our next session goes from worse to worser. How about Ave Maria University, and surprise! It's not religious? The Founder owned the local Domino's Pizza and decided to name AMU after the little town where he built the campus. Ave Maria, Florida. "You're funning me," she huffs. "No such places around here or anywhere else on the map." That was our last get-together. Eventually I did go to UGA, and it's right there on the map. In Athens . . . .

Aubergine

Bucky "the Bomb" Nichols is advised by his college counselor to add umph to his application to University of Tennessee to show he has interest in something other than football. At 6.7 ft. and 310 lbs., Bucky is a Sherman tank moving through the front line. Coach tells him he's a shoe-in for a full-load football scholarship to just about anywhere, but he can sweeten the deal if he has a non-sports-related class to broaden his academic interests and up his grade average. He is a rising senior, but there is but one class with the reputation of being a "guaranteed A or B" just by showing up and giving it a try: the Poetry Freshman Elective. So there it is. It takes two chairs and a double desk tray to accommodate the heft of Bucky's parts, and he is an odd sight in a circle of dreamy-eyed girls.

Towards the end of the first week, the shy teacher, Miss Posey, gives their first in-class assignment. She calls it "Sudden Poetry" and passes around a basket of what she, with a giggle, calls "your special topic"— each student is to reach inside and pick one subject at random. That was what they were to "think about poetically." Cogitate. Ruminate. Become fascinated with the topic. Then write a short poem about that particular subject. Bucky breaks out in hives. If his teammates find out in any shape or form that he was cogitating or ruminating on poetry in a room full of girls, he'd be excommunicated from the SEC before he even got there.

His topic is *aubergine*. Bucky has never ever heard that word. Ever. He looks around. Nobody frowns or seems bothered. Each has the look of someone floating away to join Lucy in the sky.

Aubergine. Obscene. Evalene. Elbow cream. Other bean. Austin's Queen. Barely green. Submarine. The clock was ticking. Awful scene. Crazy mean. Nice & Clean . . . .

Bucky finally decided an Aubergine might be a detergent. He begins writing.

A washing powder that gets thing clean

Don't buy Tide, get Aubergine.

He looks over at the girl next to him. She is on her second page. He tries again. It's gotta be longer.

Audi, Alfa, Acura—beware when buying a car.

Want a jazzy radio, radial tires admired near and far?

Want it with a police scanner when you want to go fast?

Travel miles and miles before you need to stop for gas?

With genuine leather upholstery, finest you ever seen?

You can have all this if you buy an Aubergine.

Nah. Bucky ruminates harder and wonders if aubergine could be something you eat. Or drink. Bucky remembers the old *Leave it to Beaver* reruns his grandmother watched, and Bucky couldn't imagine Mrs. Cleaver telling Wally and Beaver they are having "Aubergine" for dinner. So it must be a drink. He begins writing his final poem:

Go to a nice bar with your honey

Don't order beer, SPEND SOME MONEY

And if after dinner you expect to be kissed

Order two double Aubergines—with a twist.

Going around the circle, each of them, in turn, read aloud their short little Sudden Poems. The redhead with a sorrowful look said she had written a Haiku. Bucky's eyes pop open. He'd messed up. Weren't they supposed to be writing *poetry*? The redhead stood up, leaned forward and raised her voice dramatically. Her word was *rainbow*.

I am rain

he is sunshine

together we make rainbows.

Everyone claps, including Miss Posey. Next a girl, vastly endowed with what Bucky and his crowd call slammers, stands up and whispers that her topic was "wealth."

A baby robin sings on top of the shed,

A fat gray dove flies overhead.

They gather at feeders and bars

And like pooping on rich people's cars.

"My word was rich," she explains again. Nobody knows what to say so they mostly snicker. Miss Posey included. Bucky isn't prepared for what comes next from the class clown. There's always a class clown . . . . "My word is *diamond*, which is also the name of my dog."

Diamond pees

On all the trees

And on all the flowers.

She does no tricks

Like fetching sticks,

Just licks herself for hours.

Miss Posey was a good teacher. Turns out Bucky loves the class. She said he has a good imagination and there were no hard and fast rules about writing, even in poetry, and that everybody has things to say. Her best advice was "to write about something you know." Here's Bucky's final exam poem:

I'm football crazy,

I'm football insane.

I work so hard at every game

U.T.'s gonna need a huge machine

to wash my uniforms very clean,

with boxes of Aubergine

when I become a member

of their football team.

Irate

Frankie wasn't high when she picked the picture out of the style book at the beauty parlor. She was, as a matter of fact, just the opposite: low in her mind, low in her energy, low in self-esteem.

"I want it like this," Frankie told the woman whose chair she'd found herself in after a long, depressing, hard day at the Airport, where she worked in Delta Customer Services. Frankie had seen her reflection in the mirror of the Ladies as she left for home. Yikes. She looked like something from a horror movie.

She ducked in the first hair salon she came to. HairPort on 27th street, this side of her parking garage. Inside she started flipping through the *Hairstyles for Today's Woman* magazine and tore out page 67.

"You want it like that?" the hairdresser asked?

"I want it like that," Frankie said, taking off her glasses and leaning back in the chair, letting herself be covered snuggly under the plastic cape. When the woman began fingering her hair, studying it closely and comparing it to the picture her customer handed her, the massage-like touching mesmerized exhausted, downbeat, head-aching Frankie.

In a matter of seconds, Frankie closes her eyes and sinks into deep sleep. She is swimming under water, seaweed combing through her hair; angel fish and damsels cut in and out among her long curls; occasionally they would get tangled in the claws of live coral, and in this dream, Frankie can smell the salty, musky smell of the sea. Lazy dolphins, puffer fish, and prickly anemone swim with her, and once the shadow of a beluga whale blocks out the sun, making her face turn side to side in its wake. She hears the moaning and clicking sounds all whales make.

Suddenly she bumps head to head into another swimmer, a Scuba diver, who, seeing Frankie motionless on the bottom of the ocean, starts shaking and mumbling through her mask, "Frankie, Frankie, wake up now."

The hairdresser is trying to remove the plastic cape and, handing Frankie's glasses, tells her, "Time to see your new look. What do you think?"

Frankie's mouth drops open, and her eye drifts into the back of her fuzzy head. The

hairdresser had copied from the wrong side of
page 67.

Proposal

**"You can have your fancy-pants
dreams**," his mother wrote after what
happened, "but you have to put your mind into it.
If a dream is just a wish your heart makes, you're
in trouble. Life," she said, "is no Disney movie
. . . ," although across the street from our building
was a DreamWorks movie called *The Proposal*. It
pretty much bombed at the box office, but that title
pinpoints how my life blew a gasket.

I was just out of law school when I saw Sally.
She worked in the Bankruptcy department of
Casey, Casey & Casey where, so they hinted, I
was being groomed for partnership, although my
last name is Koneskilouert. Not Casey. Long

hours. No sleep. Junk food. Reading case files and law reviews until my eyes bled. Passing Sally in the hallway was the bright spot of any day. With her coal-black cock-a-poo hair, skin the color of coffee with two creams, Sally could've passed for white if she wanted to, which I hoped to God she did not.

One time, we sat at the same crowded lunch table in the Break Room. Then there was the Sunday afternoon we bumped into each other at Mamamia's Pizzeria. I didn't know anything about her job or her friends or hobbies. Or anything about her family, but I had dreamed about how swell it would be to have her around more than accidentally.

So I asked her to maybe marry me. A slice of Scarface Pizza halfway to her mouth, she laughed. Out loud. The whole place got quiet. Setting the pizza down on a napkin, she looked at me like I had asked her to burn down a church.

"Oh my gosh, you can't be serious. I don't even know your first name."

Nametag

Wooly Willy Middleton was born in Camden, South Carolina, on the last day of 1955. He was the 12th child born in the Middleton family, and the parents let the new baby's brothers and sister name each baby as they came along. This time the kids chose their favorite new toy of the year. In 1955, it was the little tablet with the outline of a person; under the cellophane were tiny metal filings that can be moved and rearranged with a magnetic wand to decorate the person.

Their firstborn, of course, hadn't had any siblings at the time, so her parents named her after that year's big news: the first baseball player inducted into the Baseball Hall of Fame. Babe Ruth. They hoped to have lots of children and were "pro-life" in both personal and political beliefs. Babies are a gift from God; the tiny embryo should be allowed to grow and be born.

A year later, they named the new baby boy Frank in honor of a Jewish teenager who hid in an Amsterdam attic. Parents stuck with a history theme with the next ones, according to the newsmakers in whatever year they were born:

Harry Truman Middleton. Lake Erie Middleton. George Orwell Middleton.

After that, the kids were old enough to pick the name of each new brother or sister as they arrived, although what they chose the first year hinted it may not be such a good idea. Hula Hoop Middleton hated her name. Next came Madam Alexander Middleton, Ringo Starr Middleton, Ford Thunderbolt Middleton, Elvis Presley Middleton, and Pillbox Hat Middleton.

Eight months after Wooly Willie was born, Mama found out she was in the family way. She announced, boy or girl, she was naming this baby herself, no questions asked, and as soon as Little Red Caboose Middleton got home from the hospital, she made a beeline for Planned Parenthood.

Spider

We called him Spider. He didn't mind, because his real name was a nightmare any kid would abandon the first chance he got. In second grade, his arms hung down almost to his knees. He started dressing in long sleeve black turtlenecks over black leotards, so the name stuck all through sixth grade when his family moved off to Los Angeles. I never saw him again. But here, thousands of miles away, my *Forbes Magazine* features an article about Elmer Uriah Meisenheimer, IV, whom editors credit with making hyperlinks embedded in URLs able to support videos on the World Wide Web.

Memory

Alice Crampton couldn't remember what happened. She'd been on stage at the

Thursday Night Karoake at Coach's Café. Halfway through "Midnight and Roses," she leaned awkwardly to the right, dropped the microphone, and fell backwards, her head hitting the wooden floor in a cracking sound the audience wouldn't soon forget.

Days later when she woke up in the hospital, she looked obviously confused, but the doctors told her family that was to be expected. Alice was awake during some of those conversations but didn't recognize any of the people in the room and didn't know why she was there.

An older woman sat in a chair beside her bed, patting Alice's hand and rearranging the covers. A young boy with red hair tried to make a joke: "Maybe this will knock some sense into your head," but nobody laughed. A man stood off in a corner and often went out for a smoke.

Going on two weeks and not much communication from Alice. Some nods asking for water. A few tears. Her eyes are mostly closed, and when open, have a look of panic and despair. The doctor declares Alice a "wait and see" case. Her parents and brother switch off, hoping for good news on their watch. A few friends come by, but they mostly talk nervously among themselves. Alice has no reaction.

Behind her oblivion and intentional silence, Alice's mind works frantically, trying to remember, to recognize, to see something that makes sense. She eventually understands her "watchmen" are her mother, father, and brother, but to Alice they are strangers; their sweet talk and constant worried look Alice finds creepy. She is, she comes to realize, in a Twilight Zone. In time, faces and places slowly begin to reassemble in her brain, and she is able to go to a step-down convalescent home and ease into her life. But the accident remains a blank.

That last night in the care facility she looked around the room where she had tried to discover herself for almost a year now. Moonlight lit up the room like a midnight sun. It turned iridescent the red and yellow roses in the hospital vase on her bedside table, and it lay like a blessing on her father asleep in the plastic sofabed in the corner, and it finally landed on her boxes packed up for going home. It reminded her of a song she once knew.

When she got home, her friends gave her a surprise birthday party at their old haunt, the Coach's Cafe. Lights were dimmed for bringing in the cake and after the off-tempo singing of Happy

Birthday, the manager turned on quiet background music.

She recognizes the tune. She knows the words.

Moonlight and roses
Bring wonderful
mem'ries . . . .

That's all it took.

Dirt

Donnie Henderson found the abandoned truck out in the woods under a mound of debris: downed trees, broken branches, offshoots struggling to get inside the missing back window.

"Well, goddamn," he whistles.

The only place Donnie allows himself to use bad words is in these woods where voices get swallowed up in wind that rattles leaves hanging on for dear life overhead.

Had he spoken at home in cursive, as his father called it, he'd be slapped full on the cheek, his mouth washed out with soap, then be locked in the downstairs closet to pray for his devil tongue. His parents feel some kind of evil egged on by his very presence and will thrash him for anything. For everything. Or nothing. The one time the school nurse calls to ask about bloody streaks on Donnie's legs, his mother tells her they are "church people who never hurt nobody." After that they make Donnie wear long pants and long sleeves to school, and the thrashings get worse.

But this truck. Good God. Holy Shit. Donnie begins to pull the trash away. It is blue, the truck. One wheel missing. Ford. Probably 1950s.

Donnie learns about cars and trucks from *Motor Trend* magazines in the "For Free" rack at the county library. He memorizes from pictures how to differentiate makes and approximate values and gets so good at it that he spends most Sundays sitting by the mailbox at the end of their dirt road, testing himself as Silverados, Sonatas, Saabs, cement trucks, and church buses roll by. He once found a Matchbox car in the school playground, but his parents throw it away because he isn't allowed toys to poison his mind with greed.

Donnie goes back to his truck the next day. And the next. It was his, wasn't it? Finders keepers; losers weepers. He patches the gaps in the floorboards, brushes out the webs and detritus from various animals' abandoned nests, sweeps away dirt inside, outside, and on top, and takes a wet rag and duct tape to the ripped leather seats. One night comes a hard rain, but by next afternoon the sun does the drying up. When Donnie gets into the woods after school and chores, the dazzling blue truck shines like it was somebody's prize on a game show.

Donnie decides to name the truck Ferris Bueller, after his favorite movie.

Donnie doesn't make friends easily and never invites anyone over from school. Nobody wants to come to a dark, dingy house with moss on the roof and so much garbage in the front yard: it looks like the house is throwing up. And what is there to do but overhear his mother and father bicker.

Closest thing to a "mate" is old Buster Wellington, who hangs around Stop 'n Go aways up the highway. They sometimes play checkers together or bet on what time Miz Fernehow will show up to buy her nightly six pack. When Donnie can't talk himself out of the need to show Ferris

Bueller off to another human being, he decides to tell Buster.

"Jumping Jesus on a Pogo stick," cries Buster when he sees Ferris Bueller under the ratty blanket Donnie uses to protect it.

Buster walks around the truck several times, pats the leather seats, traces his fingers along the lopsided steering wheel, and kicks each of the three tires.

"Well that there just dills my pickle," says Buster giving the truck a wallop on the front hood. "Let me tell you a little story. Three years ago this past July 4th, me and my cousin got pretty tanked up and drove around throwing firecrackers in people's mailboxes and open windows and stuff, until we seen flashing lights coming after us . . . the po-lice, you know . . . , so we took off faster than a topee in a hurricane." Donnie doesn't see the point of Buster's ramblings, but half the time you can't follow what he's getting at.

"We hid in these woods that night," Buster carries on as if in prayer. "Sat in my truck, fussing over how them police might be waiting for us. We decided to walk home and was planning to come back for the truck the next day, but our sense of direction was so out of whack, we headed in the all's hell wrong direction. "

Buster demonstrates, staggering around the truck, pretending to be blind. "We passed out here somewhere, and come sunup, we were so zombied we couldn't find the truck . . . , but now, Little Donnie-Boy," says Buster, hopping up and down, "you done it for us." Then to finish off the longest string of words Donnie hears from Buster, he breaks out in that squeaky dog-toy laugh of his: "This is my truck, right here."

It's getting dark, and Donnie dreads what happens if he's late for supper. Buster is still hopping as Donnie heads off. When Donnie goes back that next day, the truck is gone. He finds a mound of upshot dirt and a mix-mash of tractor-treads, obviously towing something with three wheels out of the woods toward the highway.

One Sunday afternoon, weeks later, Donnie is leaning against the mailbox, watching traffic, when comes by a blue '55 Ford with one new Whitewall and a Dixie flag fluttering out the back end.

It's Ferris Bueller. And Buster is driving.

Candy

Jimmy Miller sits in the lifeguard stand at the beach on a day that is practicing for the end of the world. Wind howls in from the west like a train making up time, and multi-colored pennants atop the rental sailboats flap like terrified butterflies.

The only people in the water are surfers bobbing up and down beyond the breakers. It's low tide so waves are as big as they're going to get, but they crest too close to shore to offer much of a ride. Jimmy never got into surfing even though he has spent his whole life two blocks from the ocean. Jimmy would rather fish. He liked the idea of surfing, but no board and nobody to do it with. He found it boring, sitting way out there, feet hanging off like bait, waiting for that perfect wave. Maybe in Hawaii or Australia you'd see more action, but here the waves are piddly by comparison: little swells hardly worth the time— and money. Both of which Jimmy is sadly lacking.

School and jobs were his priorities. He'd worked two or three jobs since sixth grade: trash collecting on the beach, everything from diapers, plastic buckets, and shovels to soda cans and half-eaten picnics left behind in the sand. Summer of eleventh grade he ran the register at the bait shop, where vacationers were willing to take home $35 beach towels with funny sayings, and kids would pay $7 for a turn on pinball machines while they ate $6 hot dogs and $15 worth of candy cigarettes and Bazooka bubble gum. He did lawn mowing, dog walking, house washing, newspaper delivering, grocery stocking, math tutoring, and car waxing all through middle and high school.

His grades weren't good enough for any full 4-year college scholarship, and his father saw no need of high education, if all Jimmy wanted in life was to fish. That was his goal: win enough fishing contests to support himself in a cheap rental, afford the tournament entrance fees, and buy gas for the refurbished junked Boston Whaler and 2004 Jeep Limited he bought with his own money.

That's exactly what he's doing now. Lifeguarding three days a week, fishing the rest. He runs for the blues every morning before breakfast and gigs for flounder at night, selling his catch to local restaurants, and he has a good deal with Captain Eddies' Deep Sea Day Trips to clean and ice up all the fish his customers bring in. It's a lonely life, but the Rolling Stones were right: *you can't always get what you want.*

The surfers are coming in now, and Jimmy locks down the sailboats and throws trash bags in the dune buggy to de-clutter the beach. He'll go home, have a beer maybe, check the news until he can't bear it anymore. He wonders if it will always be like this.

One of the surfers stops and leans against her board. "S'up?" she says. "Need any help?"

"Sure," Jimmy replies. "Thanks."

Years later, Jimmy is struck again how his life, his real life, took off by that chance meeting. Her name was Emily. She'd never learned to fish. He'd never learned to surf.

It was a marriage made in heaven.

Spigot

You know that *pssssstttttttt* sound a toilet makes when the handle won't flush? The couple sleeping in the motel bedroom paid good money to break up their three-day cross-country drive, so after the third *pssssstttt*, the wife gets up, staggers into the bathroom, feels around for the light, and lifts the plunger. The noise stops. Peace. The minute she puts the tank top back on the toilet, the *psssssttttts* starts going again.

"I can't sleep with that racket," the husband yells. Did he get up to help? No no no. His head is under the covers. He tells her in a muffled snuffle to go fix it. His exact words: GO FIX IT.

She hadn't even waked up good. People pay money to buy machines that *pssssstttttt* all night to help people do what? Sleep! A *pssssstttttt*ing lullaby. Say the power goes off during the night; they wake all befuddled because the machine cuts off. "I'm calling the super," the husband growls.

"Honey, it's the middle of the night," she says back.

Then he goes, "Well, sweetie pie sugar darling, unless you're willing to go in there and hold that balloon thing up all night, hand me the phone."

The Super arrives in his pajamas, and after some pounding and gurgling, fixes the toilet. "How bout next time," the Super says under his breath as he washes his hands in the sink, "you shut the bathroom door, put on some music and wait until morning." He leaves in a hurry and the couple immediately drifts into a noiseless sleep. Until. From the bathroom comes a *drip*. Then another. Louder: *DRIP . . . DRIP . . . DRIP.*

Silver

Baseball players have to be proficient in other things besides how to bat, throw, catch, slide, steal, and run. They must know how to spit. How to scratch. They must be comfortable wearing clunky necklaces.

This morning in the tiny print from the Sports section, I learn Carlos Abrejo quit the game. Three times he'd been MVP at his hometown high school, but after coming to the United States, now going on five years, he's still a farm team nobody. Carlos spends most innings in the bull pen, spitting sunflower seeds. His best, never good enough; even after, on his own every winter, he played pitch with a neighbor's 10-year old, gung-ho son: knuckle balls, slurves, sliders, change-ups. Every night he was at the gym: push-ups, squats, stretches—yet never saw his name on a big league roster.

The closest he got to major stadiums was watching TV. He watched Spencer Strider throw bullets 105 mph. He watched Zack Wheeler strike out people and blow bubbles at the same time. He watched Shohei Ohtani end a season with a 33.2K% rating. Carlos couldn't even brag to his little neighbor pitching buddy that he ever met any player of either team in any World Series.

Now comes another season, another chance. He scrolls through baseball re-runs on his cell phone as the Greyhound bus speeds him South for yet another stint on another farm team. Carlos suddenly realizes the one thing he hadn't done in all his game years. No clunky jewelry.

Right then and there he searches Amazon to speed-order a thick, silver necklace with a 6-inch, pure-gold pendant cut in the shape of his homeland. Two days later, he throws his first pitch on that new young farm team. The ball slams right back at him, grazes his shoulder, and knocks his expensive necklace into his mouth. With a split lip and left front tooth missing, he strides off the mound, past the dugout, through the stadium gates, into the bus station.

Carlos Abrejo never comes back to the game. Or any game. When he gets home, he rips off the chain with its 6-inch replica of Venezuela and pitches it to his little neighborhood playmate.

Voices

He lay in the muddy field and sees death everywhere he looks. The two bodies closest are both apparently still alive, but bloody beyond belief. One is an older woman, her legs at odd angles; on his other side the Russian enemy soldier seems young enough to be in short pants. He tries to remember exactly what he is fighting for. Whatever it is, he doubts it is worth this.

His sixth grade teacher had been from Russia. He himself was Ukrainian by birth and fears he may have lost most everyone in his family since the war began. He remembers peaceful times on family vacations, especially the camping trip to Lake Synevyr, one of the seven wonders of Ukraine. Their family tent had been outside Shipot beside the blue-silver Carpathian waterfalls. It was his 10th birthday.

He wonders about his brother and sister. They live in Bakhmut, where there's been nonstop bombardment, but people refused to abandon the city. His wife and baby lay under the devastation that was Mariupol. He'd left two weeks earlier to join the resistance when they bombed the Mariupol Theater, where people were hiding from the shelling. He heard that between 300 and 600 civilians were killed, including children. His child. His wife.

Suddenly a bolt of horrendous grief hits him. He wants his mother. Although she died years before, he can still see her walking in her garden:

sunflowers, lilacs, and chamomile blooming at her feet. He remembers her dinners of perogies, rolls, and on Christmas Eve, Kutia, its sweet pudding with nuts and poppy seeds that taste like heaven with a whipped cream topping. He remembers her soft laughter, how she pushed her glasses up on the top of her head whenever she had something important to say.

He curls himself into a ball to try and keep warm. He hears the Russian troops in the distance, their early victory celebrations already underway as they take weapons, watches, shoes, belts, whatever they want off the dead. He considers playing dead. Just lie there with his memories and dreams.

Their voices get closer. He sees four or five Ukrainians fighters in a last effort to stop enemy advances. In an instant he gathers himself, grabs his M4 rifle, and runs to join his countrymen.

Blue

"**Hold your head up.** Put more bounce in your step. Purse your lips and look, not bust-out angry, just perturbed. Like this." The head matron for all House of Balenciaga models strutted across the room like a flamingo over a nest of water moccasins. The new girl, hardly more than 18, looked on in growing panic. Her name was Helen Plemmons, but the powers had decided Hellzuelle suited better. No last name.

The grand New York opening was next week, and head designer Demna Gvasalia himself was to review final rehearsals in two hours. Hellzuelle (she must get used to it) tried to look smart, but all the while her mind was frazzled. If she held her head any higher wearing 6-inch patent leather pumps ($1,299), she would fall backwards and hit the runway hind-parts-before.

Every time she practiced pursed-lips in the mirror, she looked as if she were taking a whiff of cooked cabbage. And to be certain, should she up her bouncing, the silver fox manteau would slide off her shoulders and into the faces of front row patrons. Not to worry. Not to fret. After her introductory walkabout before the disciples of haute couture and haberdashery, every designer in New York was cutting out patterns for silver fox manteaus.

Fortune

After winning the contest at Good Luck & Peking Duck, I was taken on part time as its fortune cookie writer. I loved it. I had a talent for that kind of stuff, so I began putting fortunes on tiny slips of paper and stuffing them into the little slits in the folded cookies.

Don't worry about money. Best things in life are free.

The fortune you seek is in another cookie.

You are the crispy noodle in the vegetarian salad of life.

Then in a stroke of Fortune Cookie Genius:

You will die at a Chick-fil-A drive-thru in Columbus, Ohio.

(I got fired with that last one.)

Speech

Wanda O'Sullivan was in my Speech Class at Hannibal-LaGrange University. We are a private religion-focused university in Missouri, but Wanda only pretended to believe in the Bible because she was after the Good Citizens Scholarship from The National Council of Christians and Jews, so she faked it on the application. Make a choice: Christian or Jewish?

Turns out she wouldn't have known what to do with a Dreidel and couldn't tell you the difference between Simchat Atzeret and Simchat Torah, except maybe they were two different ways to cook Simchat, whatever that was. Plus the fact that O'Sullivan isn't a likely name on the synagogue membership list. Anyway, we ended up being in the same Speech 101 during sophomore fall semester.

It made you wonder about things when the professor turned out to have a slight lisp. Or, as she would say, "lithp." Busses became "buthez." Correct posture came out "pothure." And Wanda became "Mith O'Thullivan."

Time came to make our first speech. It had to be about some belief or tradition. Wanda announced hers was on the chatachisms (Thatathithumth).

At the open Q&A period after her presentation, Professor Lithp asked her about the Good Thehpard and hith theep. Suddenly Wanda asked to be excused because she had suddenly developed "hiccupthzh."

Silk

Tonight he and his soon-to-be fiancé have invited her parents for dinner at Olive Garden, where they will meet him for the first time. He'd made the reservations and hoped it was the right kind of place. Not too snazzy where a good merlot costs $20 a sip. Not hippified where you drink out of 18 oz. Jelly jars. Not uppity, where they expect you to order things you never heard of: *Fergana with Hhikilab brauns and finagling vitushi.*

But what should he wear? His blue cords with his red vest over a white button-down? Nah. Mom and Dad might mistake him for a Republican. How about his creased black dress pants and a black turtle neck? Nope. They'll figure he's the waitperson. OK. Let's think about the yellow checked silk shirt and a paisley bow tie with the striped purple bell bottoms? No no. He'd be taken for a car salesman or a loan shark.

Maybe play it safe: a dark pinstriped suit with a gray Windsor-knotted clip on? Turn himself into a Baptist minister? Or an accountant? Out of the question. If he really had his druthers, it'd be his cargo sweatpants and a Green Bay Packers hoodie, but he'd look like a gym rat, a homeless drifter who sleeps in the parking garage or someone who is partial to Michelob Ultra and beats his wife.

He finally takes a hot shower, doubles up on Old Spice Triple Odor Gel, and puts product in his hair. He's ready. He gets to her house right on time to pick her up, and she comes to the door in tiny ruffled cutoffs and peekaboo tank top. She looks puzzled. The dinner? Your parents? She rolls her eyes and rocks back on her bedroom slippers, "Honey, that's next week."

Fantastic

The women could sing. No arguing, there. They had that *je ne sais quoi,* a kind of hypnotic cheekiness that charmed the rep from Universal Music Group. But did they have the potential to play on the $10 billion UMG label?

First hurdle was their name, what they called themselves. Fantastic Five Babes wouldn't cut it. He met them at Xochi's in Houston and over a wheel of moles and masa specialties shaped into irresistible geometries (memelas, tetelas, and such). They tossed around names that might work: Virgin Voices? Fantastic Feminist? They couldn't agree on anything until the maître d' interrupted to ask if their Churros had enough cinnamon. That settled it. Spice Girls.

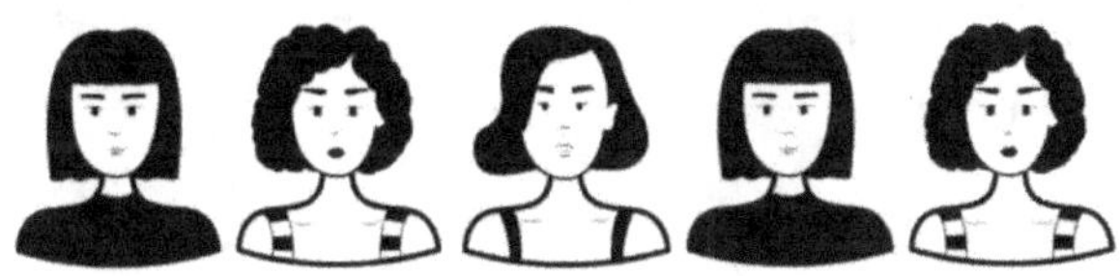

Golden

The first time Pastor Jenkins missed a golden opportunity: it turned out that the Belleek China dinner plates he found in the Antiques R Us sale bin were fake. Rip-offs. They weren't crafted in Ireland. And they weren't worth anything like $75, which is what the guy reckoned they could be. Knockoffs, the bank appraiser called them. "You'd be better off if you had invested in a set of holiday Christmas plastic plates."

The next golden opportunity to backfire came when the low mileage baby blue 2013 Kia Sportage at AutaBuy Bros. went on weekend-only sale, while Pastor Jenkins was in Montana for his second cousin's daughter's christening. So he bought it on his cellphone, sight unseen, long distance from Duluth. Put in on his Visa. A month later Kia recalled it and 1,730 others like it due to a deadly engine malfunction in the Hydraulic Control Unit.

Then came the golden opportunity to buy cheaper-than-dirt tickets to the National Roller Skating Championship at Port Fourchon. That "gold," also tarnished. Hurricane Ida made landfall near Port Fourchon, Louisiana, the day of the Derby.

All this is to help explain how when Pastor Jenkins heard Trump offer TV viewers on Shark Tank a first chance to buy stock in Bubba Q's barbecue sauce, he figured he'd learned how fate worked. There was no such thing as "golden opportunities." Only a fool would bite that shyster's golden hook. But, Bubba Q's Barbecue Sauce blew the stock market away. Its early investors are all thinking about retiring early, free and clear.

Anthem

Staff Sgt. Clifford Griswald hates bugles. "Taps" blown at a funeral makes all the women cry. "Reveille" at god o'clock in the morning is a gruesome sound. And the "Call to Retreat" nobody wants to hear.

It isn't just the military. He hates trumpets. Whether it's Miles Davis doing "Bye Bye Birdland" or Alison Balsom playing Swan Lake, Sargent Griswald covers his ears. He has to absolutely make himself rise from his seat as a bugler tries his best to give due respect to "O Say Can You See."

Gallop

Clint Jefferson gritted his teeth while the orthopedist came to his hospital room to explain things after the surgery. Not so much in pain but anger at himself for being in the wrong place at the wrong time. As quarterback at Dawson High, he had heard again and again Coach Thomas tell him to take a knee instead of going nose to nose with a center linesman. That bravado cost Clint his left elbow—and no more football ever.

"It's the worst place for a compound fracture on an arm," the surgeon goes on. "Anywhere else, it takes eight to twelve weeks before you heal, but an olecranon fracture is a break in bones that come together to form the joint. It's unfortunately possible it may never heal completely."

Clint was trying to concentrate on the dandruff in Finley's eyebrows rather than what he was hearing. Football. Basketball. Golf. Tennis. Those were the quartet gods of Clint's life. Arm-sports, as fate would have it.

After three weeks of being a sofa slug, he decided to take SCUBA lessons. There was water everywhere here in Tacoma, so why not? By the next day, Clint was in an online class; a week later he was beginning real-life dive classes with Underwarter Sports on Pacific Avenue. Clint took to it like, well, like a fish to water. The only part he did not take to at first was what to do to "prime" his mask before getting in the water: you spit in it and use your fingers as a wiper. Underwater to clear your mask, you tilt it open slightly from the top and blow your nose as hard as you can.

He fast-tracked to Master Diver Certification, and for his birthday he got a wet suit and ferry tickets to spend the weekend with his grandparents on Orcas Island. After supper, he and Granddad sat on the porch looking out on Deer Harbor.

"Have you ever gone over the Narrows Bridge?"

"Of course," Clint answered, "Hasn't everyone in the Pacific Northwest? Is it the longest suspension bridge in America?"

Granddad leaned back in the rocker and pursed his lips to pull on the corncob pipe he always kept in his pocket. It never had any tobacco in it. "Have you ever heard of Galloping Gertie?"

"No sir."

"I was three months old when the original Narrows Bridge in Tacoma opened in July 1940, and I was seven months old that November when it collapsed."

Granddad took another swig of pipe-air. "There was great hullabaloo at the time about how perfect it was, among the first suspension bridges thus far. Made it a moment in history in July for being a new wonder of the world and four months later folding up and falling into the Puget Sound. After that people and the press called it "Galloping Gertie" because it broke apart in a 50 mph wind that the towers and girders couldn't hold."

"Was anybody killed?" asked Clint.

"Only casualty was a three-legged cocker spaniel named Tubby, who got stuck in one of the cars."

But the real consequence of the event, Granddad went on to explain, were the stories that followed. Because of where it was and because of all the big pieces of bridge that landed at the bottom of the Sound, it became a perfect kind of reef for sea life, anemone, sponges, and so forth, but especially Giant Pacific Octopuses, supposedly one that grew to 600 pounds and lives there still—except that is a just a myth because an octopus can't live that long. In the 1950s there used to be octopus wrestling matches there where divers would try, mostly unsuccessfully, to bring one up.

"You know where Titlow Beach is?"

"It's a marine park near Fox Island."

"That's her, where the octopus wrestling matches took place, right where the old Ferry Dock service was when "Galloping Gertie" twisted up and fell."

People often can look back over the years and find that moment, that day, that time, which set them on their life's path. Something lit up in Clint that evening with his grandfather. He hadn't been back home to Tacoma from the visit more than a couple of hours before he checked on Titlow SCUBA Dive Shop, made reservations, and, on his way there the next day, stopped by the library for a handful of books about octopuses.

In high school he got a part-time job at the Pacific Seas Aquarium at Tacoma's Fort Defiance. Clint graduated with honors from the University of Puget Sound with a major in Marine

Biology. His doctorate from UC Berkeley earned him a research grant at the Wrigley Institute, so now he and Tubby, his longtime cocker spaniel, spend half of every year diving on Catalina Island, trying to figure out the mysteries of the giant octopus.

The title of his first book is *The Sea Monster with Nine Brains*.

Anathema

"Oh, my God. What happened to your face?"
That wasn't anything like what Wendy expected from her father when she walked into the room wearing her new make-up. It had taken almost three hours to get it right, and she'd used the new mascara pencil down to the nub.

"Oh Daddy," she says, reminding herself not to rub the itch in her eyes. "It's the new look, all the rage now. My friends are all in."

Wendy and her gal-pals at the sleepover last night spent most of their time squealing over the new *Teen Vogue* magazine and its feature on the new trendy way to use mascara: "Why be boring?" the large print italics asks readers. "Why not give your face and your makeup a do-over? Why the same-ol'-same-ol'? You can transform mascara in ways beyond its original purpose to just magnify eyes and brows. Don't be so old-fashioned!"

The article goes on to explain ways to use mascara more creatively. A *Teen Vogue* mascara guru who went by the name Divina showcased a page full of ways to give yourself "an anti-mascara look." For example, draw a zig-zagged mascara line from the upper lash line up across the forehead and then down to the brows to create a "stamped, textured look."

Wendy does her best to sound like a grownup, using a calm and deeper voice that gives no hint of the high-pitched hilarity the girls had given the idea. She goes on explaining the new mascara breakthrough to her father: ". . . or you can use the mascara 'wand'—that's what

75

they call them now—to put dotted lines across your cheeks and mouth like I did! See?" Wendy points to her nose and face while her father's eyes grow wide and he actually stops breathing.

"Next time," Wendy goes on without missing a beat, "I'm getting all different colored mascara wands to use. You ought to see the examples on the internet." The room goes quiet. Dad has balled his fist.

Wendy makes her final pitch: "Your face becomes a canvas for your creativity," her voice sounding more like a jittery 14-year-old. "You can create a different piece of art every day."

Time stops. Nobody utters a word. Wendy feels her face turning red. She swallows down the growing horror that she looks silly, that people would laugh their heads off and treat her like she was some sort of coo-coo bird if she showed up in public, but she plows on.

"Dad. Say something."

Castle

My daughter thinks her father looks like Nathan Fillion, the actor who plays Richard Castle on *Lifetime* TV every Monday night. My husband doesn't have a crime-stopper bone in his body. If some burglar bashed through our front door and pointed a gun at him, my husband would break out in hives and start reciting the Beatitudes. His body is three sizes bigger than Castles'/Fillion's. In all the wrong places.

Castle wears jeans and leather jackets, zooms off on his Harley-Davidson to solve a murder. Castle is by trade, a fiction writer, and we have trouble getting my husband to pen a short note on a Christmas card.

Castle goes everywhere with his sidekick, NYPD Detective Katherine Beckett, a smiley-face woman who plays hard to get and makes me wonder if she has ever eaten a plate of brownies all by herself standing in the kitchen past midnight. My husband wears a dark 3-piece suit and Ubers back and forth to Truist Bank as Manager of Initiatives in Execution.

Castle's mother is a wannabe actress who lives with Castle and practices her lines with him every night in the living room. My mother is an English-As-a-Second-Language teacher in a locked-down juvenile detention center, and if she lived with us, one of us would be dead in a week.

But to be fair I sometimes do eat brownies straight from the pan, and I wasn't at all hard to get once I met my daughter's father.

Dagger

I am not anti-gun. I am pro-knife. I'd never stash a loaded gun in my bedside drawer. All weaponry in our house right now is a Swiss Army Knife in the camping gear. If I lived in a sketchy neighborhood full of hoodlums, I'd get myself a real knife. A dagger. They come safety-sheath included and cost a heck of a lot less than an AK-47.

Glory

The Jones girls are playing across the street in the Salvadore's side yard, Mom watching from the kitchen window, struck by how fast her girls are growing. Martha Ann has a little swish to her hips, and Janie's snowsuit is giving her wedgies.

Eskimos, so they say, have a hundred words for "snow." Children in Rockingham, North Carolina, have only one: NO SCHOOL. Martha Ann and little Janie come shrieking down the hall this morning, "Mamma! Look outside." They make a fast job of their cream of wheat, take one sip of apple juice, and shoot outside to join their friends.

Snowfalls are rare in Rockingham, never more than half an inch, but kids make the best of it. Emaciated, medically fragile snowmen in front yards all over the neighborhood try to survive but never make it past lunchtime, leaving behind wool beanies and carrot noses soaking in a mound of slush.

Mom, still at the window, watches Martha Ann teach Janie how to make snow angels. Clay Calloway from the next block over brings a sled. Taking turns, the kids ride the sled down the driveway and into the street, while Janie watches. She knows her mom would disapprove.

When Mr. Salvador calls them all in for hot chocolate, they bust inside, leaving the sled in the crusty grass next to the driveway. All but Janie. She sits on the sled, shuffles her feet back and forth, trying to imagine what such a ride would be like.

Suddenly the sled catches the lip of the driveway, and Janie, caught in the current, heads down the driveway. Just at that moment, the UPS delivery truck rounds the corner, its driver's seat so high he doesn't see the little girl sitting, dazed in glory, in the road in front of him.

That Sunday afternoon, the church is crowded and even the preacher limp with sadness as he stands before the casket, no bigger than a camp trunk.

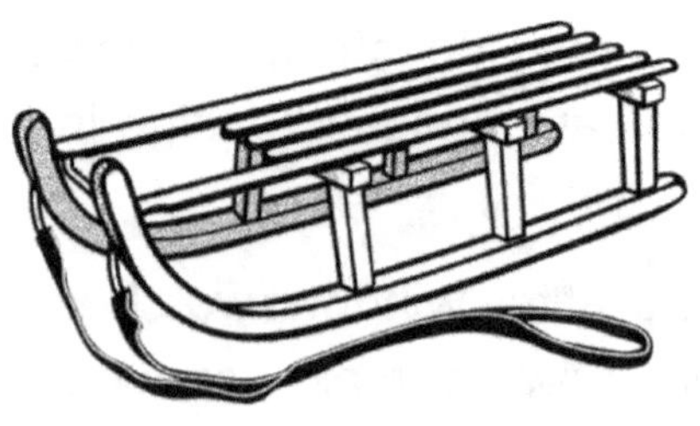

Demon

"You're such a loser," Donna shouts. "You have a sick mind."

She stomps out of the room, still talking as she disappears down the stairs: "You just wait . . . ." But even in the kitchen, Donna can hear her twin brother laughing.

Neither Donna nor Damon can tell you when it started, this battle over who could play the best practical jokes. Donna puts gravel in the bottom of his backpack. He hides under her bed until she falls asleep, then starts in a low off-and-on growl. Donna drops a packet of lime Jello in the toilet in Damon's bathroom and cracks open the window one cold winter night. He takes kitty litter, birdseed, and Elmers glue, molds it into a square that looks like Donna's special breakfast bars. She swaps the filling in his Oreos with toothpaste. And then he hides a plastic sandwich bag filled with a can of green pea soup under his T-shirt, and just as she comes down the hall, Damon steps out, heaves dramatically, bends over, and the icky green globs land SPLAT! On Donna's bare feet.

From then on, until they went off to college, she refused to call him anything but Demon.

Elevation

When Sadie and Sam Vogel opened the Saddle Up Inn on the outskirts of Santa Fe, it was built to be family-friendly and at the perfect elevation to enjoy the Sangre de Cristo Mountains. It had a pool in back, a stash of board games in the lobby, magazine racks with over 120 pamphlets on places to visit from Ghost Ranch to Roswell, free cookies in hand-painted pottery from Jackalope's. Mariachi band music and James Galway on the pan flute played in the elevator.

By the time the Vogels passed away, their sign-in books included over 5,000 names of families from Raleigh to Sacramento. By then the city had grown up around them, leaving the motel in the roughest part of town. No photo opts and nobody wanted to take over the crummy Saddle Up. For six years it sat: rot-sagged roof, dried up swimming pool filled with everything from used condoms, broken glass, beer bottles, and drug paraphernalia.

Someone had taken a paint brush and given it another name. "The Saddle Down Inn."

Plump

On her first day working the counter in Belk's cosmetic department, Viola comes home smelling like Midnight Poison, Giorgio Armani, and every number Chanel ever bottled. Old as she is (68), she is amazed at how many women worry about how they smell. On her break Viola passes time at the fingernail polish kiosk, reads the explanation of colors: Gouda Gouda Two Shoes. Teal The Cows Come Home.

One day a customer comes in to buy some plumpering aids.

"Beg your pardon," says Viola.

"Plumpering," the lady repeats.

Viola is bumfuzzled. She excuses herself to consult with a coworker who shows Viola a tube of Best Overall Lip Injection Maximum Plump Extra Strength Lip Gloss. $99.95 plus tax. "It nourishes, hydrates and makes your lips bigger," the coworker explains, seeing Viola's cornball expression as if she is looking at a bowl of haggis.

She hands Viola a *Why Plump?* brochure. "Give your lips that just-kissed feeling with just one swipe, it says. Lip jellies volumize your lips with Hyaluronic Acid." Viola purses hers. Sounds like something you put in a lawnmower. She reads on. "Full lips have always signified youth and femininity. Evolutionist prove big lips have high mating potential."

Viola sneaks a long look in the mirror after she reads the last sentence: "One of the most visible signs of aging is a pair of thin and flat lips."

Viola sucks in her lips and mentally measures them, top and bottom.

"Before you get away," she whispers to her coworker, "are there any cheaper brands?"

Frost

Billy Gibbs is trying to grow a beard. He sees the way Minnie looks at Grayson McManus, and Billy has yet to get enough nerve to ask her out. "Grayson is so manly," the cashiers at the Quick Stop chatter during their smoke breaks. "That gorgeous beard, be still my heart. So sexy."

Sexy and manly is something Billy is not. Nothing about him says "Adonis." Legs skinny as baseball bats, ears fit for a mule deer. As stock boy—whoever says stock man?—week after week Billy shelves X-large bags of dog food, brings in truckloads of watermelons big as dinosaur eggs, single-handedly hefts up from the storeroom cases of beer, bottled water, baby formula, and energy drinks.

Still his muscles refuse to bulge. And look at him now. No beard after five weeks of not shaving. All he has to show is little patches of facial hair that look like hoar frost. He buys a thing of Rogaine, slathers it on his chin. No beard. He takes special Testosterone Booster Supplements. No beard.

The day after Minnie comes in wearing an engagement ring, Billy goes home with a bottle of Wild Turkey and a new pack of double-edge razor blades.

Scratch

If you lived in England in the 1740s and had a hex put on you or stumped your toe on the foot of the bed, you would blame it on Old Scratch. Not the Devil. Old Scratch was the name of the Bad Guy back then. Words are finicky. They keep changing. *Scratchy* evolved from the Middle English "Scrat"—defined as "goblin" from the Old Norse *skratte* which meant "monster," which goes back to High German *scraz, scrato, satyr,* meaning "wood demon," and later borrowed by the Polish to indicate "imp."

See what I mean? Most words have to be put in context to know what you're talking about. Just ask the dictionary. "Scratch" has many meanings, as a noun and a verb: remove, itch; it's a kind of iron, a little piece of cloth, something you do in a game of billiards, or what happens when mosquitoes attack.

Say the word "fluke." What are you talking about? A kind of fish? End parts of an anchor? Fins on a whale's tail? A stroke of luck?

A lot of words take up half a page or more in Webster's to define all the things that one word what means. Strange, isn't it, that *polysemous* just means "polysemous."

Celestial

"Let's call her Celestial," my husband says. I'm not even showing, and he's talking about names.

"Honey," I say back, "I'm so busy throwing up, I can't think about that right now."

It's as if he doesn't hear me: "She's going to be so beautiful. So good, so heavenly. An angel, little Celestial."

I run to the bathroom, but I can hear him still talking. "We could call her Celeste. She'd be a princess, all in pink, curly reddish blond hair, tiny little pearl-toes . . . ."

I ask him to please bring me a jar of sweet dills, and is that bacon I smell?

"Celeste. Little baby Celeste . . . ," he is off in another world, ". . . she'll have pigtails and frilly underpants, sit in my lap and play with my beard . . . grow up to be sophisticated, classy but not snooty."

I can't stand it anymore. "Would you please hush, and how do you know it's a girl?"

He doesn't even stop to take a breath. "Don't be silly. Do you know any boys named Celestes?"

Eight months later we had an 8-ounce baby boy we named Buster.

Shallow

It is hopeless. How can I concentrate on homework when over my iPods comes the Lady

Gaga-Bradley Cooper duet they did at the Oscars:

> In the sha-ha, sha-hallow
>
> In the sha-ha, sha-la-la-la-low
>
> In the sha-ha, sha-hallow
>
> We're far from the shallow now.

Isn't that great? So meaningful. I remember the argument with grandmother two nights ago when she came for the holidays. Up in my room, Eminem is on my boom box, max volume, doing "Godzilla." He gets to the part where he goes,

> Blood on the dance floor . . .
>
> moon shines like Ice Road Truckers . . .

and Gran blazes through the door, waving her arms and moving her mouth: "TURN IT DOWN."

What happens next is a singalong about what is and what isn't real music with sensible lyrics. I suggest Black Eyed Peas and "I gotta Feeling." She wants to hear it, so I sing what I remember:

> *Monday, Tuesday, Wednesday and Thursday*
> *Friday, Saturday, Saturday to Sunday . . .*

She looks at me like we are of different species. "What does that have to do with black eyed peas," she asks.

I change the subject: "What's one of the songs you listened to when you were a teenager?" And she starts going on about tutti frutti and a guy named Rudy.

Good Lord. I move on to Lil Nas X, Coldplay, Pink—and Gran has a smell-bad look the whole time. One more try. Something quiet. I know she'd like Bebe Rexha. I start to sing,

I'm good, yeah, I'm feeling alright

Baby, I'ma have the best f*ck . . .

Oops. Oops. Oops. Under the tree that Christmas, nicely wrapped, is a CD of The Mormon Tabernacle Choir. From Gran, with love.

Accident

It all began the day Becky Vinetti was elected to the Safety Patrol. She would wear a plastic badge with a big orange star and a matching orange baseball cap. She proudly showed her parents a list of her responsibilities: monitor hallways between classes, keep order in fire drill lines, and stand at street corners to control traffic and make sure students crossed safely.

"No way!" said her mother after hearing that last one. "No No No." Mrs. Vinetti decided to get right on it. That afternoon she Googled "Crossing Guard" on her iPad.

The next day, an accident happened on Becky's watch. A boy on a bike zoomed around the corner, tires screeched, the kid landed on the curb, the driver of the car came out screaming. Becky's mom didn't bother to knock on the principal's office door. "The position of School Crossing Guard is one of the most dangerous jobs of all," she said, grateful for her research. "Right up there with lumberjacks and coal miners." Mrs. Vinetti was on a roll. "Over the last decade, the accident rate for crossing guards has increased by 65% . . . ."

From that little office in Merry Mount Middle School, Mrs. Vinetti's outburst—quoted and expanded on—traveled to the police chief, the mayor, Washington PTA headquarters, the School Board, newspaper reporters, and into the ears of Sunday School teachers, pediatricians, guidance counselors, and every pastor, priest, rabbi, minister, Mullah, and Imam within 100 miles.

The upshot? In a matter of months, guarding a school crossing was a job for men and women with blue headgear, silver badges, and neon-red flashing patrol cars.

Creation

Nowhere in the *Book of Beginnings* do we hear elaborations from the Genesis story. Sea creatures on the Fifth day. Land creatures on the Sixth. The Old Testament tells us God commanded in a large voice, "Let the earth produce all kinds of animal life: domestic and wild, large and small," and it was done.

That's it. Not a whisper of backstories. Were crabs born walking sideways? Was God physically in Southeast Asia to make a Borneo elephant? And we're still wondering which came first in the poultry department. Might it be possible, for instance, that the Evil One snuck in the Workshop during the sixth day while the Good Lord was at lunch; so it was He, not God, who came up with cockroaches?

There are bound to be lots of footnotes in creation. Like, maybe one of the just-minted forest animals came back with a complaint. "Sir. You've done me a terrible disservice!" Let's suppose this particular forest creature is of the weasel family: sleek body, stubby legs, small ears, thick tail.

"So what's the problem?" Yahweh asks.

"My skin! it's rough and prickly. It stabs my back and shoulder. I can hardly walk, it's so painful."

Just the day before, which would've been a Thursday, God had finished his lineup of sea creatures. Being worried about self-survival in earth's newly formed kingdom, God endowed them with shells, fins, tentacles. Now came time to fill up dry land. Still obsessed with self-protection, The Maker of All Things had originally given this little weaselish thing an armor of barbed wire bristles. As God is about to send the barbed-wired fellow off to fend for itself, it goes into a wretched heebie-geebie itching fit. Feeling remorse, the Good Lord removes the barbed wire skin and replaces it with the smoothest, most beautifully soft, and, as it turned out, most expensive fur in all of creation. The Mink.

Sister

"Tonight Sue, Brad, Tommy and I went to see *Sparkle* at the Bijou." Julianne is in the midst of reading her old diaries from back in 1976. She remembers that old picture show, scene by scene. Three girl singers from Harlem aim to be a smash hit on Broadway. They call themselves The Sister and Sisters, but they weren't actually siblings. Sister Lynette gets on drugs and dies. Sister Delores falls in love with a rascal. Sister Irene eventually goes out on her own and is sort of famous.

Life is strange and funny, Julianne thinks to herself. Last year, Hollywood came out with a remake of that old musical, this one starring Whitney Houston. Julianne had tried to get together with Sue, Brad, and Tommy, for old times' sake, maybe see it together, but they are too busy with teenage grandchildren of their own. So, Julianne went with her sister.

Earbuds

The word "loud" used to make me think of Aflac TV Commercials or five-ladder fire trucks, but if you have teenagers, it might have to do with music.

My son William bought, with his own money, a woofer and a Boom88 for his car.

Now he's asking for Christmas something called a Massive Audio Porsche Boxster Drone Video. He's got a good job afternoons and weekends at American Music Supply, so was able to put down $750 for a 2008 Hyundai.

Next thing he bought was a stereo. He wears Airpods to high school, listens to music non-stop at his job, and when he gets home, it's all hours. Before supper, during supper, after supper, doing homework, until midnight and beyond. I worry his ear canals are going to end up clogged with rock, pop, hip hop, rap, jazz, razzmatazz.

William is a good son. I can't complain. I will miss him when he goes off to university. He wants to major in Music Marketing, a career that will earn him well over $100,000 a year. For starters.

Maybe it's time to tighten that knot in the apron strings.

Trampoline

Bobby Fairchild still has the scar.

It was his 4th birthday and every mother in Mrs. Saunders Class at Playland Preschool was out to get the Best Party Ever reputation. Pony rides, clown acts, bowling rinks. Sally Grantchester had real tattoo artists come and give each child a fake tattoo of their choice. Pinky Dillard hired a make-up specialist for the girls and a college quarterback for the boys.

Meanwhile Bobby Fairchild's mom lay awake nights wondering how to compete with these. His father's only suggestion was "buy balloons, make some cupcakes, play pin-the-tail-on-the-donkey, and leave it at that."

The invitation to Betty Barnhart's party was on the kitchen bulletin board, and Bobby's mom was beside herself. They were all going to the Atlanta Zoo for a nature scavenger hunt. How does one do better than that?

The day of his party, Bobby could hardly sit still, so wide-eyed he was about the fun to come. A real British Double-Decker was to take them to the Upsy-Daisy Trampoline Park near the airport, with a stopover at the control tower to watch airplanes take-off, while eating free banana splits. Upsy-Daisy would be closed to the public, and kids could bounce all afternoon. Back on the bus home, they would serve hotdogs, chicken nuggets, pizza, and Kool-Aid Jammers. Word got around and every child (and their mother) wished they were Bobby's best friend.

But years later, ask each of those little party goers what they remember, and it wasn't the trampolines, the airport tower, or the Kool-Aid Jammers. It was when Bobby bounced so high he hit his head on a ceiling beam, and an ambulance came to rush Bobby and his mother to the hospital.

Fourteen

Kelly was just a baby when we moved into a 3-bedroom split-level with a big backyard. For his 3rd birthday he got a puppy. Best we could tell from the shelter folks: a child-friendly boxer-beagle mix with maybe terrier or dachshund. Heinz-57.

They'd been right about being good with children. By the time Kelly was 4, they were inseparable. Wherever Kelly was, there was Fourteen. We'd let Kelly name his puppy, and at two, "14" was the biggest word he knew.

When Kelly went off to kindergarten, Fourteen whined nonstop until the carpool dropped him home. At meals, Fourteen sat under Kelly's chair and thumped his tail until something "accidentally" dropped on the floor. We tried the no-feeding-from-the-table rule, but what can you do with such a cute dog? And kid.

Early one Monday afternoon, that year, the doorbell rang, and there stood a woman holding a dog in her arms. It was Fourteen. "I tried to stop, but he came running around the corner so fast . . . ." Kelly was inconsolable.

We buried Fourteen in the corner of the yard. I lay down with Kelly at bedtime. He hadn't stopped crying all afternoon. Evidently the dog had wiggled through the kitchen door while I was out, and I hadn't noticed because Fourteen usually slept in the glider on our sunroom porch until Kelly got home.

"Does Fourteen know he's dead, or is he somewhere looking for me to come get him?" Kelly asked, his breath coming in hiccups.

They don't write about this in baby magazines. I'm no child psychologist or grief counselor. I had no idea what I could say that would help. "When someone dies," I began, "like grandmother Helen did, you remember, God takes them to heaven . . . ."

"But she was old." Kelly broke in, ". . . and she was in the hospital. I don't like God very much . . . ." He couldn't even finish his sentence.

I tried again: "I've always heard there's a special bridge God built just for dogs and cats and other animals . . . ." I was winging it, but Kelly was way ahead of me.

"How is Fourteen supposed to find the bridge? He's stuck all by himself underground?"

Surely there was some eschatological quote I could come up with, but all I wanted was to comfort my sad, sad boy. "God will find him with special miracles God has for taking care of people who die. And animals."

"When?" Kelly cried. "How long does he have to stay in the dirt before God gets him."

Everything went silent. His breathing and mine. I said the first thing that came to mind. I told him It takes three days. Kelly settled down after that and I rubbed his back until he drifted off.

Next day he sat on the sun porch and didn't have much to say. We emptied Fourteen's water dish, filled it with birdseed, and set it outside. Kelly made a big sign with the number 14 and put it on top of the mounded up grave. He wanted to make sure God could find him.

After supper on Friday, Kelly came screaming into the kitchen, covered in dirt and throwing at me the garden trowel he was carrying.

"He's still there," he shouted. "Fourteen is still there. I dug him up. You just made up the stuff about rainbows and bridges. You lied!"

We didn't get another dog for a couple of years. We decided it was not a good idea. And I expected Kelly would feel disloyal.

We were at the beach when we found a little dog wandering around the sand dunes at the inlet. No tag. We asked around and for two weeks ran an ad in the newspaper. Kelly asked if she was ours now.

We said yes, and Kelly named her Fifteen.

Salad

Cow Poker is the iconic game played on long car trips, but in my family we played Bad Food Combinations. Steamed oysters with chocolate sauce. Fried chicken gizzards with boiled peanuts, fresh Brussels sprouts, and buttermilk.

Once when my parents came back from a trip to Florida, the five of us made a delicious looking, surprise welcome-home cake. It looked quite pretty, like something from a nice bakery. But it wasn't store-bought. It was concocted from our evil little minds. A joke-cake made of sawdust, Crisco, vinegar, and iced with Colgate toothpaste, the words "we missed you" spelled out in tiny slices of canned pimentos.

I am nowhere near a James Beard semi-finalist or quotable nutritionist. The only cooking-wise claim I can make is that I kept five people alive on a regular basis: husband, kids, myself. Even some four or five dogs, two cats. Oh, and the Guinea pigs, goldfish, parakeets, Easter biddies, and one ferret.

But I do now occasionally watch food shows on cable TV, and it amazes me how far we have come in the salad department. A salad back in the 40s and 50s meant a leaf off a ball of regular lettuce, a canned peach half, and a dollop of mayonnaise. Or a Jello something with canned fruit and dollops.

Today, anything goes. Just scrape out the refrigerator, chop everything up, throw on some ranch dressing. And maybe some feta.

The word "salad" comes from the Latin word for salt, but I don't know too many people who put salt on lime-green gelatin or blueberries and avocado.

By the way, I was a full-grown married woman with children before I ever heard the word avocado. Or Orzo. Then I learned the makings of what's called a larb salad: Ground tofu, Serrano peppers, rice flour, and fish sauce.

Think I'll pass.

Feisty

Joan Peelen, at 83, a first-time writer was exactly my age when she had just come out with a memoir detailing her life from age 5 to 82. She is from the south; we have both time and place in common.

She named her book, *Feisty*. It used to be an insult, that word. Life was very different for women when she and I were growing up, raising a family, competing in the workplace. In the 1960s the choices for women were pretty much "barefoot and pregnant" and "stay at home." Career choices? Teacher. Secretary. Nurse. At the opening of a recent TV special on 'feminism' the host asked if viewers could now even imagine a time when getting pregnant was a fireable offense? How about job security hinging on how much you weighed or the softness of your hands?

What if you couldn't open a bank account or establish a line of credit unless you had a husband or father to cosign for you? What if you had the grades to attend a top-level school like Princeton, but your gender kept you on the other side of those hallowed halls?

To believe a full account of realities for women in those days, most people have to be in their 80s to remember. Here, for example, are 12 things that women in the United States *could not do* until the late 1970s and early into the 80s.

1. Open a bank account or get a credit card without her father's or husband's signed permission.

2. Serve on a jury because it might inconvenience the family not to have the woman at home.

3. Obtain any form of birth control without her husband's permission. You also had to be married, and your husband had to agree to postpone having children.

4. Get an Ivy League education. Ivy League schools were college for men only until the 1970s and 80s

5. Experience equality in the workplace. A report published in 1963 revealed that

women earned 59 cents for every dollar a man earned at the same job and were excluded from more lucrative professional positions.

6. A woman was not allowed to keep her job if she was pregnant. This was until the Pregnancy Discrimination Act in 1978.

7. A woman by law couldn't refuse to have sex with her husband. It wasn't until 1993 that marital rape became criminalized in all 50 states.

8. Get a divorce with some degree of ease. In 1969 the No-Fault Divorce law was put in place, but before this law was enacted, spouses had to show the other party's faults and could easily be overturned.

9. Have a legal abortion in most states. (We're still fighting that one.)

10. Take legal action against workplace sexual harassment. The first time a court recognized sexual harassment was in 1977.

11. Play college sports.

12. Apply for men's jobs. Up until 1973, women could not apply for higher-paying jobs, which were open to men only. The

newspaper even had separate job listings for men and women, and the same job listing would indicate a lower wage for a female worker.

Women had to argue, march, be jailed, buck systems that excluded women from being smart or capable enough for leadership, be it church or civic club.

In the 1950s—some even before—women began to get feisty: Betty Friedan, Gloria Steinem, bell hooks, Coretta Scott King.

From 1960 until retirement in early 2017, I worked as a journalist and tried hard to defend the ERA amendment in mostly conservative readerships. It never passed. Even my mother suggested women belonged at home and should stop trying to take jobs like preachers and doctors away from men.

As more and more women became feisty, things began to change. As it did for Jean Peelan. Though always an ardent, feminist, she broke through tradition and raised the bar: "The world wanted me to nest. I wanted to fly."

An 82-year-old, first-time solo writer, Jean Peelan has been a wife, mother, civil rights attorney, model, actress, radio show host, and elected city official. In her spare time, she fosters dogs, fights greedy developers, and marches in every civil rights demonstration she can get to. She is feisty.

Jean lives in a tiny house in a tiny village in North Carolina.

Mother Goose

Last year we invited all the family for Christmas week. Six grands, ages 1-4, including a set of twins, one step-granddaughter, 13. Add two sets of parents, plus a grumpy maiden cousin who lives alone and heartily believes children should be seen and not heard.

Nobody agreed to leave their pets at home, so we had 4 barking and not-altogether-housebroken dogs, 2 smelly gerbils, plus an unsociable, fraidy-cat on its second set of 9 lives. For 7 days there were 20 live beings in our 4-

bedroom house. It'd be fun, my husband said. Family is everything. We'll make do.

Before they even got unpacked, I was ready to check into a Holiday Inn. They came in five different cars, and since we live on a steep hill, we had to play musical cars so everybody could unload one at a time to avoid carrying up all the suitcases, sleeping bags, wrapped presents, dog food, dog beds, disposable diapers, and diaper bags, toys, pillows, blankets, and the youngest two, who weren't yet walking.

I felt like the old woman who lived in a shoe, a shoe a lot smaller than the 2-story galosh Mother Goose had in mind. By supper time three of the children were already missing: one escaped to the basement with her Holly Hobby coloring book. We found the 3-year old cousins staggering like drunks up and down the driveway into the busy street, giggling.

When we finally sat down at the table, high chairs, and card tables, my husband called on our step-granddaughter to ask the blessing, but she said she didn't know any. Our 7-year-old's hand shot up: "I know one. My Cub Scout leader said it when Mom and Dad sent us watermelon on the camp out."

We all bowed in silence: "Good food, good meat, Good Lord, let's eat."

As we sat down our first grader made a serious observation. "Watermelon isn't meat!"

For supper I'd fixed fried chicken, mashed potatoes, carrots, and peas. For dessert, ambrosia, my husband's favorite. Turns out, the teenager was a vegetarian, and one of the twins announced he didn't like cooked carrots. "They make my head itch." As if on cue came a chorus of "ewwwwwws" and "yucks."

Carrot allergies, evidently, are very contagious. Everyone 7 and under had carrot problems except the other twin. "I loooooooove carrots, but I hate peas. They look like bird poop."

Ambrosia was the hit, but the 5-year-old was very suspicious of shredded coconut after her older sister told her it was rabbit hair. "Real hair," she swore. "From dead rabbits."

Bedtime was a nightmare. Nobody followed my sleeping charts. The dogs were jumpy. You could hear sniffing and snorting all night. Worse: that loud clicking that toenails make on wood floors and linoleum. The cat slept on top of the tree, silently chewing both wings off the paper, top Gabriel. The oldest insisted on nesting on the sofa, listening to Lord knows what on her iPods. We found someone inside a sleeping bag in the upstairs window seat; one or two small bodies were in dog beds.

I have to admit, though, my husband was right. Family time is greatest. There was magic in the air that Christmas, mixed in with the smell of diaper pails, dog breath, and burned toast. The living room spilled over into the dining room, the hallways, kitchen, and even the bottom of the hill. The house had exploded. With happiness.

The goodbyes took nearly three hours, counting all the time spent hugging, kissing, making promises, thanking for presents, finding shoes, chasing the dogs, coaxing the cat from the top branches. Back in the house, just the two of us, we felt sad, like we'd been abandoned. The house was settled and quiet. Only the sound of little wheels turning. They forgot the gerbils.

M.O.B.

When she was three years old, she was adorable. When she was 12, she was an acolyte at church. At 15 she was captain of the school debate team, and at 21, Homecoming Queen at The University of Virginia. Now, at 24, she is engaged, and day by day I am watching my smart, beautiful, articulate, church-going daughter become a Bridezilla poster: totally insane, unreasonable, and obsessive.

Here is one example, a conversation we had last night:

- Mom, have you looked for what you're going to wear?

- Wear where?

- Your mother of the bride outfit.

- Outfit? It's a wedding, not a Halloween Party.

- Mom, be serious. Don't wait until the last minute.

- My dear, it's what? A year from now.

- Eleven months, 17 days, 9 hours, and (she looks at her watch) 7 minutes and . . . 8

seconds . . . now 9 . . . tick tick . . . 10½ seconds.

- I best hurry, my goodness.

- Have you gone shopping yet?

- For what?

- Your new Mother-of dress!

- Honey, I have your brother's wedding dress.

- Mom, you need something new.

- His wedding was 4 years ago.

- But everybody has already seen that dress.

- So? See these bedroom shoes I have on? They're older than you.

- Buy something new to honor me. And what about shoes?

- People won't look at my feet. They'll be looking at you.

- I go down the aisle after you. They won't see me yet.

- Wedding fashion is about old, new, borrowed, blue.

- Bride Magazines have articles on the mother's outfit.

- Well, think of it this way: I'm old, the dress I already own is teal, which is in the blue family. You are borrowing from our retirement to pay for everything. Borrowed. Blue. Old? That's me. Three out of four might not put this M.O.B. on the cover of *Vogue*, but it's the best I can do. And unless you want to break the wedding-day budget to hire a stand-in Paris model in something Vera Wangish, you'll have to settle for the frumpy fashion-world-dropout what brung you into this world.

Throne

Elvis Presley died while sitting on the toilet. Even back in the day, I was never a fan, but why would the media chase that embarrassing fact and make the last mental picture his devoted see of him is on the John.

It's not that I think I am too highbrow for teenage-type music, too sophisticated for rap, too ignorant for jazz, or not Southern enough for blues. Our parents leaned us toward classical, choral, and opera. I have always felt dumb and socially awkward when the subject comes up of current hits with popular singers and bands. My family used to gather faithfully Sunday nights to watch the Ed Sullivan Show, and we saw the famous broadcast that introduced Elvis and his "Hound Dog" specialty to all of America. Parents were horrified, teenage girls fainted, and Elvis became one of the richest recording artist and movie stars on record, especially after death.

This year the top winning dead celebrity was Michael Jackson. He's followed by his late father-in-law at No. 2, still bringing in the money after "leaving the building." Presley is said to have earned some $5 million in his lifetime, which he spent most of himself. Since his death in 1977, he has earned well over $100 million. Other than "Love Me Tender," I never really got into his music or his moves, but I am in the minority, for sure. Elvis memorabilia is a big seller online and off. I see where one elderly fan has a 12-ft. Elvis Christmas tree and over 357 Elvis decorations she leaves up all year. When it comes to the King of Rock, people are crazy nostalgic. I bet they wish he'd died racing cars or tragically in a plane crash so they could fixate on something other than the King of Rock 'n Roll sitting in the bathroom on the throne.

Ballerina

Years ago I was invited to do a short presentation at the University of London. I had no family with me, so I spent my free time doing whatever I wanted. Like four hours at London's Victoria & Albert Museum, where I bought for $2.50 a poster of Degas' sepia etching *Girl with Field Glasses*.

Coming home I had a long delay in New York, time enough to go to the Metropolitan Museum of Art, where I saw Degas' bronzed sculpture *Fourteen Year Old Dancer*. Sadly enough it is his only sculpture, found and exhibited after his death. She looked so real, I wouldn't have been shocked if she cabrioled off her marble stand into Romeo's arms to dance the *Pas de deux*.

My elaborately mounted field glass girl poster has followed me everywhere I've lived since that London teaching gig, and the image of the young ballerina has lived in my mind since my afternoon at the Met.

Some years ago when we were selling our house, a real estate appraiser came to help with an asking price. We sat in the living room where the *Girl With Field Glasses* hung over the fireplace. The agent stopped mid-sentence when he saw it. "If you are selling that Degas original I know someone who'd pay whatever you ask. No doubt at least six figures."

I didn't take his offer, nor did I tell him I'd paid $2.50 for the poster; the $7 frame I'd pieced together from a salesbin at Michael's, and the double matting, cut from leftover scraps at a specialty frame shop. I mounted it myself using three feet of wire from our garage.

Too bad the guy who offered to buy it for a couple hundred thousand dollars isn't still around. I'd go for it faster than lickety-split—whoever he was!

Vision

SKUNK SEASON opens in NC Mountains . . . .

When Buford Ballenger read this news in the *Asheville Citizens Times*, he moved his box of Hades pellets closer to his old .22 above the fireplace. After supper he fell asleep in his recliner, dreams racing back and forth among memories of hunting with his brothers and father. They were all gone now: Billie Joe, Hank, and Pa, buried alongside each other in the cemetery behind Rise 'n Shine Methodist Church.

The four of them had ushered just about every small animal in the county over that Rainbow Bridge back in the day: squirrels, coons, wild turkeys, rabbits. But never in all those years had they bagged a skunk.

Buford woke with a new plan. He would add one more creature to the *Ballenger Boys Hunting Journal*. After each hunting trip as youngsters, they noted their victories, writing the date, the hunter's name, and what they had killed. The last entry was

Hank Ballenger. Age 11. Two squirrels.

Ma put them in a stew.

So down from the attic came Buford's bib overalls, camouflage vest, worn-thin brogans, and favorite baseball cap from Mars Hill College.

Next morning off he goes into the clear, crisp break of day. Rifle loaded. Hunting gear noticeably tighter, the overalls halfway up his shins, and the jacket won't zip. He sniffs. He shuffles. He searches undergrowth looking for nests, footprints, his ears tuned for skunkish noise. Nose for stink of burnt rubber. No luck. He comes home sweet-smelling and empty handed.

That night he studies the *Small Animal Huntsman's Encyclopedia*. He admits how skunk dumb he is. He'd never met one except Pepé Le Pew in *Looney Tunes* comic books.

In the first place, skunks are nocturnal. You hunt them at night. They feed off bugs and lizards and such, but these days, their favorite meals come from backyard garbage cans. That night, he waits till he hears crickets outside and feels darkness unfold around him. He puts on the night vision glasses he picked up from Dicks Sporting Goods. All night he tromps through a ghost-like maze of sumac, oaks. Sticky vines clawed at him from all sides. No skunks.

Then he heard it. Tiny footsteps. The rattle of garbage cans. He readjusted the night vision glasses and saw movement in the blurry green distance. It had a streak down its back, it had a tail, it was walking away with what looked like half a ham sandwich.

BANG! His first shot missed and startled the skunk. But the second hit, and it slumped to the ground. Buford felt that jab of sorrow he always felt, but guilt evaporated when in his head came his father's voice: "Good shot, son."

It wasn't a skunk. And he hadn't killed it.

There on the ground was a young black and white puppy, stunned and bewildered but very much alive. "Lord have mercy," Buford prayed. He coaxed the pup into his arms and carried it home, talking to it like it was a newborn baby: "What's your name, huh? I didn't mean to hurt you. You're no skunk, no sir, you're just a cutie pie . . . ."

He thawed a beef patty kept on hand in case he ever had company. He checked the little fellow for a collar, tags, but found neither. Buford put on some Nashville sounds and tried to think what to do next. Both he and the dog fell asleep before any answers came.

A week went by. Buford never knew dogs could have such personalities. He named the puppy Pepé Le Pew after the *Loony Tunes* skunk in his childhood comic books. They played hide and seek with Buford's ratty slippers, and Pepé learned to stand on his hind legs and tap dance to Waylon Jennings' "Ladies Love Outlaws." Eventually, Buford took his bouncy Pepé (Le Pew) to have him checked over. At the vets he saw a note stapled to a bulletin board: LOST DOG, it read. And there below was a computer copy of the little black and white puppy at Buford's feet. It was Pepé, only it wasn't. Its name was Buddy, and his phone number was 828.667.9924.

As Buford made the sad trip home from giving up Pepé to his true family, he felt his eyes burn, his throat close up, and a strange low hum starting up from deep inside himself. Suddenly he saw a flash of movement out of the corner of his eyes and heard a thump as the car hit something in the road. He stopped to see what had happened. It was a skunk. And it was dead.

That night he got out their hunting journal and made a new entry:

Skunk. Feb 13. Buford Ballenger. Age 71. Called Animal Control.

Poise

At age 63, Gretchen McMichels had a teenage daughter. Not "had" as in birthed. She'd done that 13 years ago, and if you're quick at math, you realize Gretchen was in the delivery room at the ripe (obviously) age of 51. The doctor joked it was a "change of life" baby.

Bingo! Mothering a 13-year-old girl is a big change, alright. Especially at her age. While her friends were going on cruises and thinking about opening an Airbnb with the kids' empty rooms, Gretchen was driving little Cindy's nursery school carpool, stepping around Barbie houses, and volunteering to be the go-to chaperone for Middle School trips to the Holly Farm hatchery, where every one of the kids clucked and cried over pitiful little biddies being fattened up on death row.

Cindy was in 10th grade when Gretchen's sweet little sidekick entered the Cave Years. Her first boyfriend snatched her away and left, in her place, a back-talking, sarcastic, non-communicative, oblivious clone. We met him the first time he came careening down the street in a Dodge Dart from the previous millennium that sounded like it had a trunk full of bowling balls.

His friends call him Stoner. I didn't ask why. Cindy fell for him like a ton of bricks, and we felt like every one of those bricks landed on us. I don't think Stoner was blind, deaf, and mute—but he never spoke to us, looked at us, or showed any sign of actually having a pulse. For those two-and-a-half years everything was Stoner-this and Stoner-that. Cindy fought curfew when we said she had to be home weekdays by supper, which she in time temper-tantrummed up to 10:00 on weekends. She called me Cruella under her breath every time she passed by, and when I was positive she was asleep in her own bed after a date with Stoner, I tiptoed into her room, leaned over the bed to smell her breath and check her wrists for needle marks.

She went through a few more crushes after Stoner faded away, but then came Freddy. Freddy was the king of manners and sweet-talk. When he passed me in the hallway or stayed for dinner, he would gush. "You look beautiful tonight, Miss Gretchen. This Sloppy Joe is delicious, Miss Gretchen."

I am, you realize, on the dark side of 65 by now. I don't know how I kept from beating him senseless with the bouquet of carnations from Kroger that Freddy would bring to me for being, in his words, "such a gracious hostess." Gretchen's father thought it was a hoot and would call me his hostess late at night.

Meanwhile, Cindy went through Oscar-winning personas. The street smart grunge look. The purple bangs period, where, if she wanted to see anything, she had to throw her head back. The hip-hop stage, when she played music so loud it made my jaw hurt and rattled the Wedgwood China in the living room etagere. Her walking-dead invasion-of-the-Zombies act lasted a while, when she never took off the earbuds but shuffled around gyrating to the beat of the god-awful stuff she was plugged into.

Meanwhile, my friends were going to college graduations and engagement parties, meeting up for tennis matches, buying new outfits, and joining gyms with money saved when children get full-time jobs and their own zip code. Cindy was 25 when she got married to a financial adviser just after her last year of law school. At 28 she had her first child. A girl. She named her Mary Gretchen. By the time Mary Gretchen graduated from play school, I was wearing Poise underwear, drooling in my recliner, and trying to remember to put my heel down first when walking.

Grandchildren are delightful, so much fun. Why can't we have them first?

Squash

Several years ago late night TV featured a woman who found Jesus in a bag of potato chips. Cameras zoomed in to show a large chip, and on both sides was a picture of a man's face, with long hair, a dark beard, and slight smile. She said it was Jesus and went on to be written up in *Ripley's Believe It or Not*.

Reading Ripley's can be a lot more disturbing than Jesus potato chips. You learn how half the people in the world, which would likely mean one of us, have hundreds of living microscopic mites in our eyelashes. And also, would you believe that some people put toothpaste on their steak? Believe it or not, a tea brewed from dead cockroaches was used to cure tetanus in 19th-century Louisiana, and here's to the man who successfully used a cement drill to remove a scary amount of earwax.

Ripley's gives folks an "or not" option, but the *Guinness Book of World Records* sends official judges to verify records being claimed. Some things require proof before anyone with an IQ in the double digits would accept. Like how in 1992 London's Paul Lynch performed 124 consecutive one-finger pushups. And another guy that same year set the record for best speed, riding a motorcycle blindfolded. In 2019, a martial artist in India hammered into a piece of wood 20 nails, using only his forehead. In one minute. It doesn't say how many extra-strength aspirins he took afterwards.

They say the idea for a book documenting such flabbergasting feats came from an Irish pub one night after a binge of drinking beer. Guinness, it was.

And as we speak, thanks to how that idea came to fruition, a man in Wales is practicing for his record-breaking deed to take place this summer. As a way to raise money for charity, he is going to nose-push a Brussels sprout 9.5 miles up Mount Snowdon. His first practice run took 50 minutes to go just a tenth of a mile. He estimates the entire challenge will take four days and at least 50 sprouts because they keep getting squashed. If he makes it, you can read about this "cruciferous crusader" in the next *Guinness Book of World Records*. Its 73rd edition.

Eyes

Opal Kenholt always wanted a brown-eyed baby. This time she is circling around her last chance. Third time's a charm, her mother-in-law reminds her, but the only baby her mother-in-law birthed is Ramsey Kenholt, whom Opal married even though her teenage romantic dreamboat always floated up from the developing fluids as more the Keanu Reeves, Sean Connery, Dr. Zhivago type.

Opal doesn't care whether it's a boy or girl. She has her sweet angel-pie Anne, 5, and rambunctious 4-year-old Bruce, one with eyes the color of fresh asparagus, the other a medium gray-blue.

Opal hopes this one comes brown-eyed. The last weeks of this last pregnancy, she walks like a duck and makes small children in the grocery store think she's why humans try not to swallow watermelon seeds.

As a lady in waiting, Opal nests on the sofa, flipping through a dusty stack of old *National Geographics*, which her Uncle Frank sent to her after he was diagnosed with fatal alcohol syndrome. Opal has blurred memories of being invited into his lap and taking in the sharp, dank smell of Lucky Strikes. Uncle Frank had to have been in his twenties back then, visiting his older sister while on leave from Korea where the Army had sent him to fight Gooks and Communists.

Come to think of it, Uncle Frank had dark eyes. Dark eyes usually mean brown. Uh oh. What if the baby not only inherits Uncle Frank's brown eyes but other Uncle-Frank-isms. DNA is like a sponge, soaking up whatever random cells it bumps into. Frank was strange. Opal tries to remember more clearly those visits, years ago, sitting on the Chesterfield sofa with him, looking through the *National Geographics*: full-page photographs of Zombie fish that lived all their lives in deep cave pools and had no eyes. Circles of bare-breasted women shimmying and stomping ancient tribal dances; wild, bloody-faced tigers pulling innards from their wildebeest victims; close-ups of spiders big as your fist.

Opal recalls how Uncle Frank cracked his knuckles as he turned each page. Her mother tells stories from his childhood when Uncle Frank was known for eating handfuls of grass and wearing mismatched shoes. On purpose.

What if this baby did get brown eyes from Uncle Frank but got other things too.

A week later at the hospital when Opal first holds her new baby Rose Marie, first thing she notices is that the baby's eye are nondescript. The doctor explains how all babies are born with nondescript eyes due to a lack of pigment. Once exposed to light, their eye-color paintbrushes get down to business and change them to blue, green, hazel. Or brown.

Opal spends the following two weeks taking back all the prayers she'd sent up, begging for brown-eyes. In time, thank God, new baby Rose Marie's eyes didn't have a speck of brown. They were two bright lapis-blue marbles

Rose Marie eventually grew up and married a deep sea fisherman she met one summer holiday at Rehoboth Beach. She called Opal in late November to tell Opal she was seven months away from being a Grandmother. "I don't care whether it's a boy or a girl," said Rose Marie, "but I've always wanted a brown-eyed baby."

Working

When people ask what my son does for a living, I have two answers. Not that he has two jobs, but I have to decide if they want the whole truth, the specifics, or just the general area. Do I say simply, he's a research scientist?

Or do I say he's trying to save the white rhinoceroses (rhinoceri?) from extinction? There are only two of them left in the whole world. Both female. There used to be a male still living, but he got too up in age to perform. Charlie—that's my son—says they tried to urge him on before he died, but sneaking up on a geriatric rhino to get the sperm and calming down the female whereby to put it where it belongs is pretty tricky.

So now Charlie says there are only two viable options: in vitro fertilization from a non-white rhino or taking stem cells out of one of the white males that could be used to produce sperm cells and egg cells. Personally I think that goes against God's original plan. Like they say, "It's not nice to fool Mother Nature," but I don't preach that to Charlie.

Charlie loved outdoor adventures, loved solving problems in formulas and engineering, so chasing rhinos and keeping fertilization charts is right up his alley. I just wish it was some animal besides rhinos. Like maybe bunny rabbits or parakeets. I always thought a rhino looks like what you'd get if a male elephant and a female unicorn became really, really good friends. I wish Charlie was out to save little koala bears or even monkeys or gorillas.

But it could be worse. Strange as rhinoceroses are, what if he were out to save the likes of some other strange animals about to go extinct: The pink ghost shark with a retractable penis on his head. The red-lipped batfish. The bone-eating snot-flower worm. The screaming hairy armadillo. The kangaroo. The hippopotami.

Also, I wish Charlie's father, rest his soul, could see him now. He'd never even gone to college, much less graduate school. My in-laws made a living growing summer tomatoes and other produce they sold at a roadside stand near Myrtle Beach. In winter my father-in-law drove a county school bus. Neither of them finished high school. How times change. Like the fact that even though Charlie's father was just a mailman, back in those days, a working father, a stay-at-home mother and two children could live off one full-time job.

You can't do that now. When Charlie gets married it's gonna mean both parents have to work full time for them to afford a place to live, buy food, a car, have health insurance, pay taxes, start a family. The woman he dates now works at Pet Smart. I hate to think the time might come when I'd have to brag about a son who helps rhinoceroses get pregnant and a daughter-in-law who worms puppies and untangles cats with hairballs.

Maybe I'll just make up something impressive like cruise captain or programmer for nuclear trajectories from Ursa Minor.

Stitch

Tina heads outside to mow the lawn when her mother calls out, "Young lady, just where do you think you are going?"

Tina shrugs, what?

"You haven't got a stitch of clothes on and you are going out in the front yard? What has gotten into you?"

Tina informs her mother that today is May 4th, and May 4th is Naked Gardening Day in America and that Asheville, North Carolina, is the third most popular place in the county for naked gardening.

Mom stands, hands on hips, face pinched up tight as a piece of hand-work smocking. "Well, not in this garden, not dressed like that . . . undressed like that. It's indecent. Go get pants and a tee shirt on. You look ridiculous."

Tina goes into one of those teenager slouches, scrunches up her face, and tells her mom that's exactly the kind of thing they've been discussing in her Feminist Thought class at school. American cultural mores, TV commercials, magazine articles, and Facebook are rampantly, purposefully, and detrimentally body-shaming women and young girls into treating their bodies with all sorts of beauty, skin ointments, and waging a war on fat . . . .

"Listen here, professor," her mother shouts back. "Pushing a lawnmower buck naked in a cul-de-sac with young kids on bicycles and grandmothers sitting on porches does nothing for women's liberation. It's tacky, it's disgraceful, it's ungod-like." Mom regrets that last word because Tina comes back with the indisputable fact that Adam and Eve were naked in their garden. It was Satan that made them start cutting out fig leaves. Mom is bumfuzzled. Anything she starts to say sounds like biblical hearsay. "Well," she says, "At least put on a sunhat."

Doorbell

Mildred Hitchcock is not a cat person. Her life was filled with golden retrievers chasing balls in the backyard, chunky black labs that jumped up and licked you when you came home, dogs that could learn to sit, stay, fetch, and shake hands. Their only bad habit was to sniff visitors in the crotch and whine for handouts from under the dinner table.

When Millie moved onto Wentworth Avenue, her next-door neighbor had a cat named Sampson that took a shine to Millie. Every time Millie came to visit, Sampson would sit on Millie's head like a Siberian general's fur hat. Millie tried to politely shoo Sampson off, but Sampson took no hints. He just turned around and hopped back up and nested in her hair.

Mildred Hitchcock is not a cat person. Late one night when Millie went to the beach with her bridge club for a weekend getaway, she and her partner were driving back from a night at the Surf Club when a cat ran out in front of the car, and they heard a slight bump. Her friend yelled out, "We hit it," and Millie slammed to a stop so hard all the takeaway boxes of leftover BBQ, slaw, corn muffins flew of the back seat and landed in a sticky mess. Her friend insisted they crawl through sea grass and sand spurs to find the probably-wounded creature, and at the top of the last sand dune, Millie, as she pulled cactus needles off her cheeks, shook her head and tried to sound sad, "Must've gotten away, so let's just pray he's safe and sound."

Mildred Hitchcock was not a cat person. When she and her husband took an anniversary cruise to see the pyramids, the tour guide said ancient Egyptians used to worship cats, which explains why they were everywhere: on roof tops, in trees, inside shops. Everywhere. In restaurants Mildred watched them crawl underneath the table, slink in and out doorways, and in open-air cafes, peer down from rafters and pee on food below. She didn't see a single litter box anywhere. She ate only packaged crackers and took a long shower every night.

Mildred Hitchcock was not a cat person. Years later, widowed and her daughter married and living in another zip code, Millie moved into a nice retirement community that allowed her to bring her last Lab who was old and crippled and bit the dust before Millie got the boxes unpacked. She now lived all alone for the first time in her long life. The children called often and she was grateful for that.

Her granddaughter in Charleston called and said she and her son were coming to help celebrate her new digs. When the doorbell rang that morning, Millie ran with glee to the door to fling it open—and there on her front steps in a beautiful Gullah sweet-grass basket wrapped in pink gingham was a tiny, white kitten. Out jumped her 4-year-old great-grandson: "Nana. Look what I brought you!"

Mildred Hitchcock is now a cat person.

Freckle

David and Douglas Jeremiah, even when they were old men, nobody could ever tell them apart. They were twins, of course. Identical. Those first few months, their mother kept a braided bracelet on each chubby wrist, green for Davie, blue for Dougie. Naked, she could not tell them apart. Neither had a distinguishing freckle, birthmark, cowlick. After two months, their dad cut the bracelets off because he thought they look sissified on boys.

Even by the time they were three, even four and five, they couldn't tell which was which. Even the little boys themselves didn't know, so Mom and Dad just figured they'd wait for some tendency or personality trait to show up and meanwhile call them whatever name popped into their minds at the time. Dougie? Davie? Didn't matter.

That's how it went all during their growing-up years in their tiny country village set in the middle of nowhere. Davie and Dougie were always together, so people weren't bothered by which one was which. They lived to a ripe old age, and nobody was surprised when they died on the same day, same time, buried together in a common casket with one headstone. They were like conjoined twins. In this case, Davie and Dougie were born separated at birth but became joined once they got here.

Snaggled

"Well. You want me to tell you how things got so snaggled in my family? I'm not sure I can, but I'll give it a go."

I am sittin' on a couch in Dr. Brinkley's office; he sits by with his ever-ready notepad and waits. This is my third visit to the school counselor because my teachers think I have "issues" and decided Dr. Brinkley needs to be called in. I am not a troublemaker, hardly say a word in class, and am an A student.

So why am I here? I think I know. Every time a teacher sends home something to be signed by a parent, a different person signs. My school record shows six different home addresses. When I try to explain, their eyes blink faster, and they bite their lips.

This time, Dr Brinkley opens a folder of papers with a different name on the line that says "parents." Yes, I have parents. My mother was a professional dog walker for folks over in Greenway Manor and places like that in the other part of town. And the day after she had me, my father (they weren't married) took a job as Fuller Brush salesman, and except for a few postcards from Cedar Rapids, Baltimore, and Disneyland, nobody ever hears from him.

Not long after, my mother went off with a fellow who traveled the country making his living from local eating contests. Four dozen oysters at a Charleston plantation, 56 chili hotdogs at Cony Island, 26 peach pies in Waycross, Georgia. She left a note with our neighborhood asking please somebody look after me until she gets back.

We live in a subsidized low-income apartment "across the track," as a couple of the bullies at school call it. But it's OK. Everybody mostly keeps to themselves, and on the 15th floor, which is my floor, we are like family. I switch off staying with different ones until my mom comes back. Nobody, including me, believes she will, but they never let on that's what they also think.

I nearly fell over when Dr. Brinkley's office door opened, and in walked several of the "parents," whose signatures were bogus, unlawful—words Dr. Brinkley made sound like it was murder instead of a signature.

Dr. Brinkley calls out the first bogus signature: Cleotis Rustyhannagan. It's a permission slip to go to city hall with the class to watch traffic court. We were the age kids start getting learners' permits, so it didn't take a brain surgeon to see the purpose of the outing.

Cleotis explains my folks were out town, and then, under his breath like he's talking to himself, says, "She don't have no car to crash. The onliest car I know of in our building is broke down and sits by the fire escape year round. Kids write dirty words all over and then sit inside to pass joints."

The next unlikely "parent" signer is Glory Angel Houston, signed on my English book review on Joseph Conrad's *Heart of Darkness* I'd written a month ago. The teacher has asked a parent to verify I didn't get help.

"Did you really come up with your comments on your own or copy them from some OTHER WRITER," asks Dr. Brinkley. "Do you remember the paper? Here's what you wrote, and it doesn't sound like someone in your grade, does it?

Never in all my life has 100 little pages made me contemplate suicide . . . violent suicide. I had to finish it. I had no choice. Every page was painful. Am I supposed to feel sorry for him? Because I don't. I feel sorry for all of Africa getting invaded with dumbasses like this guy . . . oh, and in case you didn't get it, Conrad spends many many useless words clearly explaining the layers of meaning in his title. Metaphor overkill. He's like, like, oh, man

. . . my heart is dark . . . and I'm also in the middle of Africa . . . and it's dark . . . and depressing . . . get it . . . get it?

There is a long silence. Finally I apologize for writing 'dumbasses' but, yes sir, I was really depressed by the story and wondered why we were reading it when, well, there are a lot of hearts where I live that are full of darkness."

Angel looks near tears because judging from the grimace on Dr. Brinkley's face she thinks I am in trouble.

She turns to Dr. Brinkley: "That man C-C-Conrad, Joe or wha-what-what-what-whatever . . . . I know him personally and how he is with words. He got her so upset and made her write those things. Joe Conwright, or whatever, he actually lives t-t-two floors dawn, and oooooo-weeee, you've never seen nobody crazier. If he's been telling s-s-sad stories, ain't no fault of hers. Talks to hisself all day and night about Lady Dianna and their affair, and I don't speck J-J-J-oseph C-Conway t-t-t-taken a shower in months. We try to keep chi-chi-chi-chi-children away from him. He sits ow-ow-ow-out on the fire escape if'n it g-good weather and tells stories."

Dr. Brinkley nods that Angel has said enough. He shuffles a few more papers, then asks, "Who is this Junker. It just says Junker, esq. Scribble like. We couldn't reach him, but he showed up in person and told the principal he was here for your Parent/Teacher conference."

"Mr. Junker," I explain, "is our maintenance and caretaker for the building, and he's in charge of collecting rent each month. The city rents by the month, and anybody doesn't pay that month has to move out, so when Mama left and rent came due, they rented our two rooms to Old Cady Freemont; he's blind and kinda loco. So Mr. Junker knew she'd gone off without me, so I had to stay with others who'd take me on for a while. That way nobody was stuck with me too long, feeding me and such, and sharing a sofa or sleeping bag.

"Mr. Junker said Child and Family Services would come and take me away if they knew all this, so I should keep quiet. I stay longest time with Mr. Junker—they have a foldup cot in the hallway next to the heating unit, so it was my favorite place. When they sent home the notice about teacher conferences, everybody decided Mr. Junket should be the one. Angel was embarrassed of her stutter. The Rustyhannagans couldn't be counted on to be available; she sometimes sleeps off a bad night at the police station, and he has two Doberman pinschers he takes everywhere he goes because he says he's being followed by the FBI.

"They agreed Mr. Junker knew me best cause we watch TV wrestling matches down in the basement. He's been practicing an imaginary parent conference with all the others and probably was a little nervous. He's also been on the lookout in the downtown library for textbooks so he can study for questions the teacher might ask. How did he do?"

Dr. Brinkley itches his nose, then takes the clean, starched handkerchief from his breast pocket. And blows hard. The room falls silent except for the wheeze in Cleotis's breathing. His wife tells him he sounds like the school bus coming to a stop every morning at our corner.

Cloetis tells them my favorite color, that Ms. Klowendowsky braids my hair every morning and that my favorite meal in the free-lunches counter is the green bean casserole with meatloaf.

"Well," Mr. Brinkley says finally. "Seems like we're done here. Thank all you folks for coming. And this gal here," and he winks at me, "is being raised right. She's gonna 'mount to something with this kind of family behind her. And you can count on us here at school," he stops to clear his throat, "as part of that family."

Harmony

When lightning struck the old tulip poplar in the side yard, Terry jerked awake so violently it might as well have been a bomb. She hadn't realized she'd even been asleep. Her last thoughts had been about the "two roads," as Carl Sandberg put it, now "diverging" before her, just like in the poem. A lot depended on which one she would take.

At 31 Terry was still single and still living with her parents. She was now the financial manager of the 10,000-acre dairy farm her great-great-grandfather started a hundred years ago. From six cows and a rickety barn, it was now on the historic register as a well-known tourist attraction and had turned his hardworking, ambitious progeny into millionaires. Terry's two brothers took over after dad's stroke four years ago, and Terry left her stockbroker job in New York to come home and take over the books.

Terry'd had a brilliant childhood, growing up with two brothers and a sister. Betsy lived with her husband and their teenagers, and their full-time job was managing the farm's Welcome Center and General Store.

Growing up, Terry assumed she would someday move away, get married, have a family, and spend every vacation at the farm. She'd had her chances but never said yes.

This time was different. She'd known Skip Wellington all her life. They grew up together. He was literally the boy next door. They had even kissed one summer, after racing across the Cow Pond.

The Cow Pond. Such an awful name for her favorite place on the farm. Clear deep water, shaded by weeping willows. The cows had never put so much as a hoof in that water. Story was, it had originally been dug out and fixed up as a swimming pool for children on the farm and in town, but in time the YMCA opened a public aquatic center, so the Cow Pond was mostly a scenic spot on the farm bus tours.

She and Skip had built a long bench out of leftover lumber and four large stones they rolled down from a nearby pasture. They often met there after the school bus dropped them off and did homework together. He was whip smart in language arts; she was a genius with numbers. They agreed if they were one person, they would win top honors.

They talked about all sorts of things. Which is what they were doing that day when they kissed. It wasn't romance that brought their lips together. They were trying to see if two people who had braces on their teeth would get tangled up if they kissed. The idea of their hobbling along to find an adult to use pliers and snippers to unhook them got them to laughing so hard, both went home with hiccups.

They weren't 14 now, and if Terry took that road of marrying Skip, it would mean a lot more than play-like kissing and a comfortable friendship. It'd mean moving into a different place. Sharing the responsibilities of jobs, children, looking after each other. All the hassles and disharmony of being hooked together, this time not by braces and childhood but by promises to keep forever.

Terry loved her life on the farm. Coffee with her mom every morning at the same kitchen table her grandparents and great-grandparents had used, hearing bass-note hums and barks from the milking barns. Fresh milk still warm, butter churned the day before. Sitting in her hayloft office figuring ways to save money and make money and stay in budget. Since she'd been there, profits had risen and financial worries fallen. Long evenings spent in the den with the people she loved most in the world, reading quietly or playing boisterous games of Trivial Pursuit. How could any other road take her to a better place?

But then there was Skip. Kind, gentle, easy-going, and the smartest lawyer she'd ever known. He too, loved the farm. Essentially grew up with her. They had kept close all these years, FaceTimed during college and graduate school. He was in New York for law school; they had run the marathon together. And she loved him. How could she not?

After law school Skip had married his competition in a bankruptcy case, and Terry had been Skip's version of "best man" and godmother to their first and only child, a daughter named Bonnie.

But Skip's wife was not cut out to be a mother or wife of a high-level New York lawyer, and she eventually walked out on Skip and Bonnie. Devastated, Skip and Bonnie moved outside New York, and Skip settled in as a small-town lawyer.

A week ago, Skip asked Terry to marry him. It wasn't exactly out of the blue. Two roads.

Skip was coming this weekend, and he would get her answer.

Bamboozle

"Where are we?" The question hangs in the air among three hitchhikers left standing on the I-40 overpass. Black exhaust stings their eye as they watch the truck get right back on the Interstate. They'd been physically thrown out the back of the cab, though no use to wonder why. It is hard for three men crammed in such a tight space to get into an actual physical fight, but they'd manage. One of their elbows had jabbed into the truck driver's ribs, and the driver swerved so suddenly onto the Swannanoa exit that Bucky Lee, the skinniest one of the three, landed on the floor screaming.

"Get out," the driver barks, hardly coming to a standstill. "Go on, and get out."

He'd picked them up at the Flying J Truck Stop outside Charlotte, but it hadn't been long before the lingering effects of two bottles of Jack Daniel's stolen from the ABC Store had them turn to fist fights over how to divide the $137 cash into three equal parts.

Bucky Lee breaks the silence and lets loose a string of inventive smut and says, "Let's rob something else, right here in this town. Swamnunabor or everhow you pronounce it. Use the knife we used . . . ."

Don, just grunts and breathes in short fits and starts: "We ain't got no weapons now since shit-for-brains here" (he points at Rufus) dropped the knife in the cooler while we bagged money from that register . . . ," Don snorts before making his final point, "and then when the owner comes out the men's room, we run off, but Rufus here forgets to pick up the friggin' cooler . . . , so we ain't got no knife to point and no beer to drink."

They begin walking. No one speaks until Bucky Lee sees the Dollar General. "We could get some kind of weapon in there. And something to eat."

"Yeah, genius boy," says Don. "Let's find a late-night gas station in this itty-bitty town and threaten the cashier with a Dollar General dustmop or a bouquet of plastic geraniums. And ain't nothing more satisfying than a Dollar General can of Vienna sausages that expired in the previous millennium, and for dessert, how 'bout some Dollar General breath mints?"

They walk on, turn down a twisty side road running along a creek bank. It's dark, which suits the three, but after a while they come to a U-Haul center all lit up with, seems like, hundreds of rental trucks strung in rows across the lot. They go inside to use the men's room and pass several vending machines in the lobby.

They carry paper bags, one with bills, one with of all the nickels, dimes, and quarters lifted out of the cash registers in the liquor store they robbed. They use the loose coins to load up on popcorn, M&Ms, Junior Mints, root beer, and Slim Jims.

Ducking low, Don, Bucky Lee, and Rufus crab-crawl through the parking lot of U-Hauls and find one in the farthest, darkest corner, open it, hike themselves in the back, and eat their junk-supper.

It isn't long before the three are all straddled out, sputtering, gurgling, and snoring loud as a moose in heat. Hours later, Bucky Lee jerks awake first: "Hey y'all. I think we's on a train." The others raise their heads.

Big Don rubs his eye. "Bucky Lee, your IQ is lower than room temperature in an igloo."

They bump along in silence, when all of a sudden they hear water beat against the sides and top of the truck, and a gust of a growling wind hits so hard they fall sideways.

Bucky Lee, nervous as a cat in a room full of rocking chairs, grabs ahold of Rufus and spit-whispers, "Oh, my soul and body, it's a hurricane. Whaddarwe-agoonna do?"

Don jumps up and unlocks the U-Haul latch while shouting over the outside noises, "Run. Fast as you can."

It isn't a hurricane roaring against the truck. They are in a drive-through car wash, and just as the three tumble out the back of the truck, two revolving brushes swallow them up and spit them out into a rainstorm of soap suds.

As fate would have it, when Don, Bucky Lee, and Rufus stagger out of the 150 MPH dryer winds, they bump right into a Highway Patrolman waiting for his car to be polished and the sack of money falling, bill by bill, out of a soggy wet paper bag.

Their bam had been boozled.

Leaves

A mica-colored sky lets in the morning light. Wind whips through trees outside her bedroom window. It is mid-December, and only a fistful of twisted brown leaves still hang on. The rest have fallen, then blown away by grounds crew at her assisted living. If she could reach out and pull off one of those stubborn left-behind leaves, she'd be tempted to congratulate it for hanging on. Or should she pity it? But the word that comes to her as she imagines holding it up to the mirror light is "transparency." Old leaves are transparent, broken through in places. She can see to the other side.

She's no biologist, but she knows dead leaves decompose themselves and in time recompose into nutrients that work together to bring new life, come spring. So goes the parade of seasons and the cycles of life.

She herself is in the autumn of her years, though never overanxious about what is to come when she lets go, as all leaves—and humans—eventually must.

She has regrets, of course, and roads taken or not taken that sadly or gladly changed the shape and boundaries of her days. Now those times sit like brambles pushed to the side as she rides through the currents of 83 years of happy memories.

And she herself has become transparent. There's nothing she can hide, really. Her balance, her need for quiet, her unsteadiness, the reaching for common words and familiar names that now play hide and seek. The only thing not going under cover is the explosive pride and unspeakable joy she has in her children and grandchildren—that is who she is, and always has been, at her core. Nothing else matters as much, and it's something becoming more apparent, more obvious than ever in her long life.

She laughs at herself for the clumsy philosophizing, her gloomy poetics, and she cusses the arthritis and shortness of breath as she pulls herself up and off the bed. See how transparent she is? She's not fooling anybody. You know right away she's an old geezer. Still holding on.

Peaceful

In the land before time King Botox and his son Adivan ruled for 20 years of calm and quiet after defeating the Codines and razing their capital city, Pepto Bismal. Without battles and devastation, the warrior-like Viagras turned their energy and inclinations into sporting competitions called The Ozempics. Peasants and priests from as faraway as Wellbutrin gathered in outdoor arenas called Amoxicillians to crown the winners and reward them with their very own NyQuils. Popularity of these games roused jealousy among their neighboring kingdom of Meta Mucil, famous for its mighty army, led by Captain Hydrochlorothiazide. Softened by years of gardening, Scrabble, and other peaceful pastimes, the city of Xanax succumbed to the Advils, and damned by the great and powerful Witch Hazel, all peace-loving citizens of Ambien were banished to the wastelands of Opioid. The End.

Fire

We paddle the five miles down the Indian River through a gallery of moving fresco paintings. Black gum trees, willow oaks, tulip poplars, and evergreens crowd together like vigilantes up and down either side of the dark denim river. Below our campsite, two humpbacked boulders sit side by side along the shoreline like woodland creatures lapping water from a clay dish. We hear gulps and gurgles as fish settle in for the night. The sun slips away in the afterglow of daylight; the sky goes mad with colors until a pitch-black blanket drops down over everything. We gather wood and put up our tent, listening as logs pop and hiss until suddenly they catch, throwing a fistful of flames into the night.

It's early October, and here in upstate New York, fall begins to whisper what is to come: leaves will sail off to do their part in the parade of seasons, and air will change from musty summer heat to the mint-like flavor of winter. We hear the lullabies of loons from nearby weeds and rushes, the quiet rhythm of waves blessing the shore. Scenes and dreams, wishes and wonder play in our minds as we sit in that spooky, splendid silence, together, by the fire.

Afterword

According to the *Oxford English Dictionary* the one word with the most meanings is "set," which has 430 separate definitions. Every year new words become legitimate. Recently, we added 690 new words to the English dictionary: Rizz (charm), zhuzh (small improvement), simp (longing), cromulent (acceptable). The longest word in English is the name for a certain protein— 189,819 letters.

Who decides what a word means?

Like Humpty Dumpty, we make up meanings. A grandmother sends a note to the teacher that excuses little Susie from school the past three days because she was "naustecated." A 3-year-old sleeps in his "janamanas." Mr. Dumpty would be pleased to know our language is being more and more liberated. Slang and invented words are not as looked down upon as with past dictionary guardians. "Blamestorming" explains itself (trying to figure out who's most to blame when a problem arises). "Cellfish" is what you call someone who pays more attention to their phone than the people in the room with them. "Chiptease" is when your chip bag contains more air than chips. My favorite is "gallinippers," defined as extra-large mosquitoes, and an "ultracrepidarian" is in the dictionary as "one who gives opinions on something beyond their knowledge."

Disney's *Mary Poppins* let us believe supercalifragilisticexpialidocious was made up on the spot by Julie Andrews, but it dates back to the late 1300s when it meant "surprising." Mary Poppins pretends she just pulls it out of the air as something to say when there's nothing to say. Like when the cat's got your tongue. Which is pretty much how I'm feeling right now.*

*ancient kings would punish those who displeased them by cutting out their tongues and feeding them to their pet cats so they would be left without words.